# The Whooten Forest Mystery: Ties That Bind

Copyright 2025
Chistell Publishing
https://www.chistell.com
First Printing, September 2025

Published by:    Chistell Publishing
                 7235 Aventine Way, Suite #201
                 Chattanooga, TN  37421

Author:          Denise Turney

ISBN: 979-8-9856651-9-2

## Dedication

For my son.

I love you, Gregory –

## Chapter One

*Fog seemed to be on her attacker's side, because where it was hard for Petula to see -- the sound of his feet landing against the ground swiftly, absent hesitancy -- her attacker was moving easily, cutting through the underbrush with haste. But Petula refused to give up, running with her arms swinging wildly, her legs churning up ground, tall grass knifing her ankles.*

*She pushed aside drooping tree limbs, creating a narrow path through the woods as she ran through the dense fog, desperate to reach the nearest open sand road. Her breath caught in her throat. She gasped and pushed forward, racing against time, eager to widen the space that separated her and the stranger chasing her.*

**\*\*\*\*\*\*\*\*\*\***

She'd first seen the man, a bushy salt and pepper beard covering the bottom of his face and a black and red bandana wrapped about his head, while she had been backing her class A recreational vehicle into a parking spot at New Jersey's Whooten State Forest campground.

Two brown and white Basenj dogs, their ears erect, short tails curled, had stood on each side of the man. They followed him as he came within inches of her RV. She'd been studying the area through her RV's rearview mirror, checking to ensure that she wasn't about to back into trees or someone's pet.

"I can spot you," he told her, his alto voice gruff, yet gentle, kind.

She turned away from him and rolled her eyes, as sweet a brown as her skin. "No, thank you." A series of heart-breaking relationships and living alone in Atlanta, Georgia had made her fiercely independent and more cautious of strangers; watching true crime TV series only deepened her distrust. It had reached the point where her friends told her that she was going to regret being overly independent and cautious. Although they cloaked their perception in humor, Petula knew that her friends sincerely meant it when they teased that she was far too solo-strong, too committed to the single life. And yet, when she looked at the man a second time, instead of accepting his help, she twisted her mouth and rolled her eyes again.

As if he hadn't heard her, he came closer to the RV and started tapping his knuckles on the vehicle's front side, just below the driver's window.

"Said I don't need anyone to spot me," Petula repeated, a deep frown roughing up her forehead, her husky voice generally animated now booming and hard.

"I've backed my RV into a parking space on my own many times."

The strange man smiled, revealing his cracked, stained teeth. "Got one of those backup cameras, do you?"

Punching the accelerator, she sped her black and gold RV backwards, inches in front of a row of trees. Normally, she would have exited the vehicle, to check for scratches and to retrieve parking levelers out of the bottom storage area. Yet, there the man stood, unwilling to move.

Checking that all doors, including the emergency roof exit, were secured, she stood and walked to the back of the RV. When she caught the man looking through the large side windows, his gaze pinned on her, the smile he'd once wore gone, she pulled the black shades down.

She listened to the sound of leaves crunching underfoot as the man walked away from her vehicle. Relief she felt could be heard in the thick breath escaping her mouth.

The relief, though sweet, was short, quick like a sprinter's thrust.

The man sneered, his voice threatening. "I'll be watching you."

Fear turned into anger. She'd traveled to the area to visit with her friends, Gloria and James, a couple she'd known since college. No way was she going to let this strange man run her off. Despite what the man may have thought, she told herself that she didn't owe him her time. On top of that, if he was attempting to flirt with her, she thought he was doing an awful job.

"Men," she sighed. During college and her early working years, Petula's life had been filled with a string of broken relationships, men she'd given her heart to lying to her while they tried to hide painful affairs. Her last breakup had come two years ago, with a man who she had dated for three years, a man who'd abandoned his romantic relationship with her colleague, Veronica, to start dating her.

Now single and to avoid further heartache, Petula vowed to never fall in love again. Armed with a master's degree, her life was filled with work. On top of logging 60 to 80 hours a week at Custom Accounting Designs, she volunteered on weekends at a housing company that built homes for families facing homelessness. Her schedule had become so full that she scarcely found time to travel to

Ohio to visit with her sister, Ariana. She needed this trip, downtime to rest, relax, and have fun with her friends.

The strange man's last words echoing in her mind, she hurried to the front door and yanked it open. "What?" she screamed. In an instant, her anger subsided, turned into shock. She stepped back and gasped when she saw a familiar keychain hanging out of the man's pocket. "Custom Accounting Designs," she whispered, leaning forward, staring at the keychain. Looking at the man's head, she made out a bright green Army patch sewn into his bandana's top right corner.

Seconds later, her gaze fastened on the man's dogs. Glancing away from the dogs, she told the man, "I don't know you. Mind your business. Leave me alone."

The dogs snarled, their jagged teeth showing like hard, sharp blades, eager to draw blood.

As if starving for a fight, the man let go of their leashes and the dogs sprinted toward her.

Petula pulled the door closed, but not before the dogs slammed into the RV, barooing and growling.

Half an hour passed before she opened the front door again, climbing out of the luxury RV and retrieving the parking levelers out of the bottom storage bin, refusing to be imprisoned by the man's threats. "I haven't done anything to him," she mused. "I don't even know him, and I'm not about to spend my vacation hiding in my RV or anywhere else." Plus, she was no longer alone.

During the half hour that she'd been hiding in her RV, two Fifth Wheels, a van and another Class A had parked to the right of her RV. On the left side of her RV were acres of forest and a narrow path that led to a place yet unknown to Petula. Six kids played in an open area at the front of the vehicles. Watching the kids play brought back memories of the fun she'd had playing as a kid with her sister, Ariana, and their best friends, Trisha and Bernadette, so much so that she smiled.

She inhaled deeply, her shoulders rising then expanding as she admired the area, bountiful with tall trees, underbrush, waterways and wildlife like black bears, coyotes, wolves, raccoons and bobcats.

"Hey," a tall, slender woman, her red hair pulled back in a ponytail, called out. She was looking at Petula. Before Petula responded, the woman started walking in her direction, a smile lighted upon her blemish free face. "My name's Ashleigh." Looking over her shoulder, she said, "And that's my husband, Byron. The shortest of the six kids playing over there are ours, two boys and a girl. We went into town for groceries earlier today."

Petula backed away from Ashleigh still shaken from her encounter with the strange man.

"My family loves to camp," Ashleigh smiled. She opened her arms and turned from side to side, admiring the landscape. "Nothing is as amazing as nature."

"Yes. Yes," Petula nodded, being drawn in by Ashleigh's kindness. "And what a beautiful family," she said, looking at Ashleigh's kids playing thirty yards away. She shook Ashleigh's hand. "My name's Petula."

Ashleigh kept smiling. "Just getting here?"

"Yes. Pulled in about half an hour ago."

"It's gorgeous out here. We've been at this campground for five days. Think you're really going to like it."

"I'm just passing through on my way to Bensalem. Want to check out Newtown and the summer shops there. You can find the cutest trinkets, souvenirs and fashions, not to mention the good food at those summer shops, items that are hard to find anyplace else. I also want to get to Neshaminy State Park while I'm in the area. But really, I'm going to visit with friends."

"That's what I love about RVing," Ashleigh said. "You can travel, catch the best sights and visit family and friends without thinking about hotel costs."

Petula nodded. "True."

"While you're out here, make sure you use good insect repellant. The ticks and fleas are bad, especially this time of year."

"I figured as much about the fleas," Petula said. "It is June, but ticks." She scrunched up her face. "Wasn't counting on having to deal with ticks." After a pause, she said, "Speaking of things to look out for, during the five days that you've been at the campground, have you seen a guy with a beard and two dogs around here?"

Ashleigh shook her head. "Can't say that I have."

"He was here when I pulled up half an hour ago."

"Oh," Ashleigh laughed after a pause, tugging at her memory. "I think I know who you're talking about. He's always wearing a bandanna?"

"Yeah." Petula chewed her bottom lip, recalling the keychain, then she asked, "Does he work around here?"

"Don't know. Like I said, we've only been here for five days. Every time I've seen him, he's been in this area or off this hiking path. There's a prohibited sign in front of the off-grid hiking path. At least three times, I've seen him walk back in the area until I couldn't see him anymore. He's handsome, looks like a tall James Dean. Another thing – he always has those brown and white dogs with him. I think they're Basenjs. Those dogs are great hunters, and I do mean great hunters. Because of the way their larynx is made, they don't even bark, making a long baroo sound instead. People call it barooing. They're very protective of their owners. If you have small pets, keep your eye on them."

"I don't have small pets. But is that guy cool? Is he okay? Do you know him?"

"No. My husband and I have seen him around here maybe five to six times over the last few days. He's always by himself with those dogs." She shrugged. "He doesn't bother anybody." Suddenly, Ashleigh laughed. "You're not single, are you?"

Stepping back, Petula waved her hand. "Oh, no. It's not that at all. I'm not hardly looking for a man. I already have one," she lied.

Ashleigh laughed. "Well, good for you, because there isn't a lot out here as far as high-quality available men goes." She searched Petula's face, noted her furrowing brow and the squint in her eyes. "But back to the guy, as far as I know, he's okay. His name is Paul. At least, that's what he told Byron and me. I haven't heard anybody else say anything about him. He seems to know this area well." She shrugged. "He might be from here."

Shaking her head, Petula said, "He asked if I wanted a spotter when I was backing in—" She rolled her eyes upwards, then waved her hand. "--Never mind." She shook her head, sending her black, red and green beaded earrings swinging from side to side. "It's probably nothing."

"Why don't you come over to our RV tonight? It's the green and yellow Fifth Wheel over there," Ashleigh said, glancing over her shoulder. "We're cooking out and we could play a good game of cards with you and some of our neighbors."

Petula grinned. "You all don't play for money, do you?"

"No," Ashleigh laughed. "We just play for fun."

"Okay," Petula smiled. "I'll be there."

Out of the corners of her eyes, she spotted Paul peering around a bend at the back edge of the campground, about two hundred yards from where Ashleigh and she stood. "Maybe I should move my RV closer to yours," she said, glancing toward the campground's back edge.

Ashleigh followed her gaze. "Let me go get Byron. We'll help you get moved, and don't worry. We'll keep an eye out for you. Paul's probably harmless, but it never hurts to be careful."

Fifteen minutes later, Petula's RV was parked within twenty yards of Ashleigh's and Byron's, and Petula was breathing easier, not taking in quick, shallow breaths. That night, she enjoyed playing several hands of spades with Ashleigh, Byron and two other couples. While the adults played cards, the kids played tag and rode their bikes in the open area in front of the RVs. The scent of the hot dogs and seasoned hamburgers the adults had cooked on the grill earlier lingered, attracting fleas and gnats.

Most of the insects got caught in the bug lamps hanging at the side of the Fifth Wheel. The sound of the insects buzzing as they hit the lamps was drowned out by the pop, rhythm and blues and country music playing on the iPod at the edge of the folding table that the couples played cards around. The music, card playing, and conversation relaxed Petula. "I was overreacting about Paul," she leaned back in the folding chair and mused, smiling at the two aces and King of Spades she held in her hand. "Everyone here is nice. There's nothing to worry about."

Byron threw in his last hand of cards, then stood. "Kids, are you ready to head inside?"

"No," the kids laughed.

"Well, you're going to have to head in soon."

"When?" a red-haired boy who looked no older than six-years-old asked.

"In about five minutes. How about that?" Byron asked. "Is that long enough for you to play before you head in for the night? We can watch one of your favorite movies when we get inside." Peering at his son, he smiled. "Sound good?"

"Yes," a snaggle-toothed girl with plaits in her hair grinned.

Petula stood before the kids hurried inside the Fifth Wheel. "Thanks for inviting me over," she said, looking from Ashleigh to Byron to the other couples. "It was fun." Although she tried not to, she glanced toward the edges of the campground. Her breath caught in her throat when she saw what looked to be a man with two dogs standing behind a van.

Ashleigh and Byron followed her gaze. A second later, Ashleigh stepped toward Petula. "Gotta second?"

Petula glanced at the van. "Sure."

"Let me run inside our Fifth Wheel and get our business cards. Byron and I work remotely doing marketing work for startups and mid-sized companies. Our email addresses and our cellphone numbers are on the business cards." She looked at Petula. "I'll be right back."

While Ashleigh ran to get the business cards, Byron made small talk with Petula. "You're a pretty good cardplayer."

Petula smiled. "I've played a few hands of spades in my time."

Byron laughed. "It shows."

Ashleigh hurried toward them. "Here are our business cards," she smiled, handing the cards to Petula. "Like I said, our email addresses and cellphone numbers are on the cards. Don't hesitate for a second if you need anything." She glanced at Byron. "We're happy to help."

Byron nodded. "Yes. Call if you need anything. We're right next door."

Petula tapped the business cards in her palm. "Thank you. I really appreciate it." She looked at the van. It was still parked about two hundred yards from where their RVs were parked, but this time when she searched for Paul and his dogs, she didn't see them. "Here's my cellphone number," she said, scribbling her number on paper she'd torn away from one of the business cards.

She looked at the van and told herself not to worry. She handed the strip of paper with her cell number on it to Ashleigh, then she turned and walked, one cautious step after another, toward her RV.

Chapter Two

An uneasiness, a nagging sense of danger, crept over Petula when she looked at her levelers on her way inside her RV for the night. "Looks like the back leveler chocks shifted," she said aloud. Glancing over her shoulder and seeing Ashleigh and Byron chatting outside their Fifth Wheel, she started walking around her RV. As she made her way around the vehicle, she bent toward the ground and returned the chocks to their original position. When she reached the front of her RV again, she stepped back feeling relieved; shaking aside thoughts that something was amiss, she looked at the leveler chocks and told herself, "A forest animal must have bumped into them."

Climbing the three exterior steps to her RV, she entered the vehicle, cellphone in hand. "Jambo, Ariana," she smiled, greeting her older sister, the woman who had been her best friend since they were kids.

Since elementary school, Ariana and Petula had been each other's trusted ally. They stood up for one another, proclaiming the other's innocence whenever one of them found herself in trouble with their parents. They played hopscotch, hand-clap games and double Dutch jump roped with each other and neighborhood friends. They plaited each other's thick, coarse hair and capped the ends of the braids with colorful barrettes, orange being Petula's favorite color and purple Ariana's. They looked at each other and beamed, "You're beautiful" when they put on their mother's make-up and clonked around in their mother's too-big-for-them shoes. During their teenage years, they shared details of crushes they had on neighborhood boys.

Before she left Atlanta, hitting the road in her RV, Petula had called Ariana, assuring her that she'd let her know when she arrived in New Jersey. Glancing toward the RV's kitchen sink, she told Ariana, "I made it to the Whooten State Forest."

"Is it as beautiful as you thought it would be?"

"It is," Petula beamed. "A lot of people come here to fish. There are a lot of good hiking trails here too."

"Would love to be there with you," Ariana said. "Not that being in hometown Ohio eating the best locally cooked pizza you can imagine isn't a good thing."

"Are you at a restaurant with your hubby, Leon, and my two sweet nieces, Mara and Paula -- one of those popular restaurants mom and dad used to take us to when we were kids?"

"Yes. Guess where we are?"

Petula eyeballed her refrigerator, knowing there was no pizza inside, wishing she was with Ariana. Turning from the refrigerator, she guessed, "Mitchell's Pizza in Columbus, Ohio."

"You got it!"

"Eat a slice for me."

"Petula, this pizza is so good. I'll eat a piece for you and two other people," Ariana laughed, the familiar hoot that reminded Petula of home, the laugh she'd smiled at or joined, rolling in her own noisy merriment, reminiscing about their childhood in Columbus.

"Remember when Mama and Dad would take us to Mitchell's Pizza when we were kids? I always got extra mushrooms and extra cheese on my pizza," Petula laughed. "So much cheese that pizza looked like it was stretching when I bit into it."

"We'd get all those toppings, then pick off the tomatoes," Ariana giggled.

"And have fun riding those small rides at the back of the pizza shop. It was like a place for adults and kids. We'd eat two slices of pizza then hurry to the back of the restaurant and hop on those rides then fall asleep in the back seat of the car when Dad and Mama drove us home."

"Edward Mitchell definitely was a smart business owner."

"Yes," Petula agreed. "And he was a nice guy. So many people from Mama's and Dad's high school graduating class became entrepreneurs who kept that friendly hometown approach to their businesses."

"You know," Ariana said, "Maybe that's why Mama and Dad brought us to Mitchell's Pizza – what – like twice a month. They probably got price deals on the pizza and pasta we ordered, being that they'd grown up with Edward."

"You could have a point," Petula chuckled.

"Speaking of good times, when are you going to hook up with your friends, Gloria and James? After all, that's why you drove up there, right?"

"Yes," Petula nodded. "Wanted to get back up North, visit with Gloria and James. We haven't hung out like we did in college since we graduated. We used to have a blast at college football and basketball games, especially those big championship games. And on weekends, Gloria and I would hit yard sales. Gloria knew how to grab decorative scarves, fashion pins, belts, jewelry and hats at yard sales and match them up with boutique blouses, dresses, jeans and dress pants. Talk about a great ensemble. She was a fashion genius. And we had so much fun, laughing until I thought my sides would burst, while we hung out at local late-night diners."

A pang of regret rose within her, revealing itself like a surprise. It had been several weeks since she'd felt guilty for not visiting family and friends more. Since she'd made plans to travel North, she'd imagined the fun that Gloria, James and she would have, making the trip a highlight of her summer. "I've been trying to keep in touch with all my friends better." Looking at her hands, she told Ariana, "Gloria, James and I will connect soon. They're in Florida right now. They'll be back in a few days. I wanted to come up early and hit a few spots on my own, not to mention get away from work." She shook her head. "I've been working crazy hours. I really needed to get away and rest."

"What are Gloria and James doing now?"

"Gloria works at a venture capital firm. James works with a hedge fund."

After clearing her throat, Ariana asked, "Are they in human resources, marketing, legal or another support function?"

"They're middle managers, overseeing accounts."

"Similar to what you do," Ariana said.

"Not exactly," Petula shared. "Remember, work I do focuses on the insurance sector."

"Remember when you lived in Bensalem, near Philadelphia, while you were attending college? I always loved the times I visited you there, the trains going to New York City, Maryland and Pittsburgh make getting around easy. There's so much to do in that area."

"Yes, but I haven't been up here in years, spending most of my days exploring Atlanta and the Southeast, not to mention visiting with you, your beautiful family, Mama and Dad and everyone in Ohio."

"So, are you going to get out and explore the forest or head to Newtown?"

"I'm going to explore the forest and hike one or two of the trails first. I have time to shop at the boutiques in Newtown. I'm looking forward to going there too."

"Bet you're glad to be away from that Veronica at work."
"I am."

"She sounds like a bully. I think she's jealous of you."

"She does bully, but not sure she's jealous. She holds her own at the office. She's a good worker, smart, sharp. Talk about a stylish dresser. Veronica only wears the finest designer clothes. She aims to impress. Not sure what her deal is. Like I told you before, I recently discovered that the last guy I dated used to be Veronica's boyfriend. The three years he and I were together, not once did Veronica mention that I was dating the guy she'd once dated." She shook her head. "And he never mentioned it. Not sure if she holds that against me even though I didn't know they had been together when he asked me out, but I'm glad to get a break from her. She's always on me, pointing out mistakes I make, it doesn't matter how hard I try or what I do. And she stays on top of client files like you wouldn't believe. Veronica knows clients, especially the bigger, influential clients. Some of them consider her like family. They trust her. She's been handling some of their personal files for years, even helping them with estate planning."

"Who cares how many people trust her. No one's special."

"Didn't say Veronica was special, but she's won insurance sales representative of the year five times. Plus, she's the only sales rep at Custom Accounting Designs who's earned a master's degree in insurance management and another master's degree in actuarial science, not to mention that she's been at the firm for years. She's been there a lot longer than I have. Plus, I heard she started small, like I did when I first entered the industry. She had to make her own contacts like I did. She worked hard to get to where she is."

"After all you've told me about her," Ariana said, shaking her head, "there's something about her that I just don't trust."

"Heard Veronica had to cut corners to get a break years ago," Petula sighed, unwilling to accept deep misgivings of the woman whose career start had been so like hers. "Word on the street is that, regardless of how hard she worked when she first got in the industry, she couldn't get ahead, something she really wanted." She shrugged. "Who knows? If our parents were different and hadn't raised us to be so honest, I might have turned out like Veronica." Her voice lowered, softened, trailing off as she looked out across her RV's driver's seat. "As much as I might not want to admit it, I know how to go after what I want too." Sighing she added, "As Mama and Dad used to say, where there's a lot of money, there's deceit and trickery. Big business is ripe with corruption." Sighing again, she added, "Guess Veronica figured she had to get slick to get ahead, and so," she shrugged, "that's what she did." Taking in a deep breath, she continued, "I just want her to stay out of my way. I just want her to leave me be."

Gazing at the floor, Petula recalled her last interaction with Veronica before she left for vacation. She had been walking out of the firm's large boardroom, surrounded by a dozen colleagues.

"That was a long morning briefing, wasn't it?" Veronica had asked Petula, bumping her shoulder.

Surprised at Veronica's effort at light conversation, Petula nodded "Sure was," and kept walking.

Standing a sleek five-feet-ten-inches, Veronica opened her stride and quickly caught up to Petula. "Got a second?"

Petula stopped, her navy-blue cotton poplin dress hanging loosely across her shoulders. "What do you need?"

Raising her black leather executive briefcase close to her mouth, Veronica dropped her smile. "I think it's best we speak alone." After a pause, she laughed, "I think it's best *for you* that we speak alone."

"Okay," Petula sighed, turning and entering a small conference room. "Let's go in here."

Following Petula inside the conference room, Veronica closed and locked the door. Then she hurried across the room and pushed the chair Petula had pulled away from the table against the desk edge. "Listen," she frowned, pointing at Petula. "Stay out of my business."

Petula stepped back. "What are you talking about?"

"Stop looking through my records. Stay away from my clients."

Waving her hand, Petula laughed. "I'm not trying to get information about your clients for my own personal benefit." She frowned. "I know better than that." Shaking her head, she added, "All I'm doing is gathering information for the audit, work that's part of my job. I'm only doing my job." Rolling her eyes, she told Veronica, "Besides, the audit's almost over."

Veronica pressed her nose against Petula's forehead, invading Petula's personal space absent concern. "The audit is being called off.

That was less than a week ago.

Pressing her cellphone against her ear, Petula looked to the top of a cabinet, at a framed collage of family pictures. "Veronica really got pissed at me about a week ago."

"Why?"

"There was an audit." She sighed, stunned at how Veronica seemed to be set on undermining her career, accusing her of snooping through her client records for personal gain. "But what really pissed Veronica off is that one of my clients had called asking to make a change on one of her accounts. I looked and looked through my records but couldn't find her file, the one for this account with her signature on it. So, as a last resort, I looked through Veronica's files. And - walla – there the signature file was. Something looked off about records I saw." She waved her hand, hoping to erase her suspicions about details in Veronica's work that she'd discovered during the audit. "But that's not your problem."

"No. Tell me. You're my sister. Whatever you tell me is safe with me. Besides. Who could I tell?"

"It's nothing. The numbers just looked off." As she sat on the RV's sofa, she told herself not to think about work. But the numbers she'd seen in Veronica's files troubled her, not to mention the fact that her client's file had wound up in Veronica's office. Shaking her head, she added, "Not saying I haven't ever forgotten something, but I just don't remember making those changes to my client's file and I definitely didn't put my client's file in Veronica's office."

"What changes?"

"It's nothing," Petula tried.

Ariana refused to back down. "Petula."

"There was a 1A charge on some files," Petula told her, eager to change the subject.

"What's a 1A charge?"

"It's a code for a chargeback the firm rarely uses and should rarely use."

Ariana laughed. "Why are you being shy? Sounds like you don't want to talk about it. Is this code some big national security secret?"

Shifting on the sofa, Petula bit down on her bottom lip before she told her, "Ariana, I created the code about two years ago." She released a thick breath. "There's so much regulation in the industry, such long paper trails. The code can potentially eliminate the need to create a long paper trail for certain transactions. It saves the firm time. It saves the firm money, but it can cause extensive financial damage if misused.

Silence, a rare interlude when the sisters were communicating, separated them. Then, Ariana asked, "Did you know Veronica when you worked in Custom Accounting Designs' Bensalem office?"

"No, but she has strong contacts all over the insurance industry."

"I don't care how well connected she is or how powerful the clients she works with are, you're a good employee."

"Yeah. But, like everybody else, I make mistakes." She sighed. "Thinking back, I probably left my client's file on the copier and Veronica accidentally put it in her files." Shaking her head, she said, "She never messes with my files."

"Don't make excuses for her having your files or have a soft spot for her just because she started in the industry the same way you started, on her own, without contacts, having to learn the hard way. You must look at her the way she is now."

"I don't have a soft spot for her, but she did help me better understand the inner workings of Custom Accounting Designs when I first arrived at the Atlanta office." Releasing a deep breath, she added, "Veronica was nice to me back then. She kept telling me that I reminded her of herself when she started out, sharp, a newbie to the Atlanta office, but willing to learn." She laughed. "Back then, I was like a sponge, soaking up everything she told me. Then, I started earning my way and getting accolades and Veronica started to change." She shrugged. "It was like she wanted me to always be the student."

"More like she wanted you to stay in her shadow," Ariana frowned. "Did you tell Veronica your vacation plans?"

"Heck no," Petula screamed. "No way."

"So, she doesn't know where you went?"

"No."

"Good. You don't want her calling the Bensalem office, giving you grief from there or coming up with some emergency work issue to make you come into the office while you're in the Northeast."

"The only person I told was my manager, Arthur. Oh," Petula added, "and I told the receptionist at the office. She's cool."

"Good," Ariana nodded. Seconds later, she said, "Well, Sis, I know you'll have a blast on vacation. Wish I was there with you. Maybe next year, we can vacation out of the country together. You've been talking about visiting Canada and Africa for I don't know how long."

Petula smiled at the thought of vacationing abroad with her sister. "Let's start making plans to go before we talk ourselves out of it."

"You're on," Ariana said. Then she passed her cellphone to her husband, Leon, and their two daughters so Petula could speak with them.

Ten minutes later and no longer talking on the telephone, Petula spent the next hour watching *The Vince Martin Show*, one of her favorite comedies. Afterward, she enjoyed a warm shower and headed for bed.

The night was uneventful, except for the sound of insects hitting her RV windows. Paul crossed her mind a few times but knowing her gun was in her top nightstand drawer helped to ease her nerves, so did the numerous prayers she prayed throughout the night, especially times when she thought the forest had become too quiet. The few instances the keychain flashed across her mind, she squirmed in bed and reminded herself that Custom Accounting Designs was a national firm that gave away branded items such as keychains, pens, drinking mugs and baseball caps to customers living across the country, including places like Bucks County.

It surprised her how soon morning came. Despite her earlier concerns about Paul, she woke feeling as if she had gotten five hours of deep sleep, on top of another two hours of light sleep.

She was sitting at her RV's kitchen table eating scrambled eggs when her cellphone buzzed. When she picked the phone up, she was surprised to see that she had a text message from Ashleigh.

*"Byron, the kids, and I headed out early this morning. Late last night, we got a call that Byron's mother was in an auto accident. She's okay, but we're on our way to be with her. You'll figure your way around the area. Don't worry about Paul. Like we said, he's probably harmless. But if you are still concerned about him, just go to the campground management office during the day. They're closed at night. Just let them know you're concerned and why. Enjoy visiting the Newtown shops and hanging out with your friends. – Ashleigh"*

Petula stared at the text message. "Nice of Ashleigh to send a text, especially after what I told her about Paul," she nodded.

Dismissing the fact that Ashleigh and Byron were gone and eager to learn more about the area, she left her RV, her handgun in her shoulder pocketbook, and walked around the campground after she finished eating and cleaning up. She stayed outside for an hour, not once spotting anyone who looked out-of-sorts.

"This place is beautiful, so peaceful," she thought aloud when she returned to her RV and climbed the steps. "But I'm not staying here as long as I had planned."

It took her less than half an hour to prepare the RV for travel, in large part because she hadn't taken down many dishes, clothes or personal hygiene items when she'd pulled into the campgrounds yesterday. For that, she was grateful.

When she went back outside to remove her levelers, she was surprised to find the chocks were gone. She walked around her RV, looking beneath the vehicle for the chocks. After she reached the front of the RV, she gasped. She ran her hand across the hood. "Damn it," she cursed, surveying the forest. "I've got to get out of here," she said, raising her hand and smelling the fluid. "Smells like somebody poured anti-freeze onto the front hood." Pulling a towel out of her back pant pocket, she wiped the hood clean.

Hurrying inside the RV, she climbed behind the steering wheel and turned the key. The engine was choppy, then it made a gurgling sound, a noise she hadn't heard before.

She banged her fist on the steering wheel.

For the next several minutes, she worked to start the RV. Finally, she called an emergency RV repair shop. She was relieved that she'd kept the number in her cellphone contacts.

"You smelled anti-freeze?" the technician asked Petula.

"Yes. Someone poured a lot of anti-freeze on the hood. I wiped it off earlier when I was checking my vehicle."

"Are you traveling with kids?"

"No, and kids wouldn't do that."

"Well, then I'm not sure how the anti-freeze got there. If too much anti-freeze got in the engine, it could cause a problem. Hoods on those RVs are tight though. Doubt much anti-freeze got in there. Check the wires," the technician told her over the phone. "Sounds like your RV isn't getting enough voltage. I bet you the RV will turn over after the engine gets enough juice. It was running perfectly when you bought it, right?"

"Yes."

"What company did you say you bought it from?"

"I bought it brand new two years ago from Outdoor Travel."

"Outdoor Travel is a good RV company. I'll hang on the phone. Get out and check the wires. I can walk you through it if you want me to."

"Please do," Petula sighed. The first thing she did when she exited the RV was to look around the campground. It surprised her to see only one Fifth Wheel. There was no other vehicle in sight. Her heart sank when she saw the Fifth Wheel owners packing to leave.

Embarrassed to bother them, troubling them with her fear, she hurried to check the wires. She laughed to hide her unease when she saw that the wires were loose, almost unconnected. "That's what it was. The wires must have bumped loose while I was driving on unpaved roads when I first got out here at the state forest," she told the technician. "I'm new at RVing, only hit the road about four months out of the year. I'm still learning."

She closed the electrical cover and nearly ran back inside her RV. "Thank you," she told the technician. "Do you mind hanging on until I get the RV started?"

"Sure."

"Oh, my goodness," she sighed when the RV's engine turned over. "Thank you so much," she gushed, relieved to be moving again. Moments later, she was on the sand road, headed out of the state forest, the thick trees and an eerie growing silence pressing in on her with each passing mile.

## Chapter Three

Thirty miles through the state forest, the RV sputtered and the familiar gurgling noise, choppy, jolting and annoying, returned. Although Petula was certain that her RV's engine had created the sound, she looked out the window, hoping to discover another vehicle struggling to keep speeding down the road.

There wasn't another vehicle. As had been the case for the last eight miles, she was alone. Rubbing her hand across her forehead, she twisted her mouth, fighting back a tinge of disappointment. Aloneness at the popular state forest wasn't what she'd expected while she'd clicked through outdoor review websites, campground directories, and the official Whooten State Forest website from her Atlanta townhouse.

Her love of being outdoors, hiking mountain trails, fishing, grilling on a fire pit, and chatting with other campers and hikers stretched back to her childhood. It started with her Girl Scout membership. She and her classmates who were in the scouts went on weekend camping trips close to their homes in Columbus, Ohio.

Back then, Petula especially appreciated the taste of grilled hot dogs and hamburgers sandwiched between a thick, soft bun. Girls in her troop would stay up late at night, darkness surrounding them, playing games and telling each other ghost stories. Feeling scared, their eyes big, their shoulders hunched as if shrinking from certain danger, their hearts racing -- felt like fun then, but they'd all been together, not alone.

Years away from her Girl Scout days, looking through her RV windshield at miles of open state forest road and acres of woods for bears, wolves and bobcats to hunt prey in, Petula cursed. "Damn it. I should have just drove right to Bensalem or gone straight to the Neshaminy State Park. It's safer there, not nearly as much woods as there are here." Staring at the open road, she moaned, "What was I thinking when I decided to come to this state forest?"

She thought about calling her sister, Ariana, but figured there wasn't much she could do in the way of help being that she was hundreds of miles away in Ohio. "Just keep going," she told herself, pressing down on the accelerator.

She'd been driving for twenty-five minutes, sticking at five miles above the posted speed limit. If the road had been wider, she would have driven faster, fed her desire to be away from the area and the growing sense that her vehicle might leave her stranded miles away from the state forest management office, a gas station or another public establishment. Mixed in with her fear, like an injurious lesion, was Paul's threat. She'd also started to again wonder who had taken her leveler chocks and poured the anti-freeze on her hood.

Men like Paul had crossed her path before, but it had been years since she'd encountered a man who brought up so much fear within her. The last time she was afraid of a man to the point of becoming anxious was ten years ago. She'd been at her apartment in Bensalem, Pennsylvania.

Evening had been settling over Bensalem, the place where she had lived for several years, a suburb twenty minutes north of Philadelphia, a place she had been happy to call "home". Earlier that week while she'd been outside walking around her apartment complex, she'd walked by a man's apartment.

The man looked to be in his fifties. He had enough hurt and rage in his face to let a stranger know that his had been a hard life. A week later, while she was watching TV in her apartment, she felt a sinister presence on the other side of the door. At once, images of the man surfaced in her mind. She was certain that it was him.

Whoever it was stood on the other side of the door for ten minutes. It felt like the longest time to Petula. To be certain that her mind wasn't playing tricks on her, she'd even crawled quietly to the floor and looked beneath the door.

There they were – two sneaker clad feet standing still, as if their owner couldn't make up his mind whether to barge against the door, trying desperately to force it open, or turn and walk away. Petula prayed while she waited for whoever was on the other side of the door to leave.

After the man left, as she often did when she was troubled, she'd called her sister. Talking with Ariana relaxed Petula, made her feel safe. But the experience with the man standing outside her apartment door had changed her, took something away from her. Sitting behind her RV's steering wheel, her mind searched for other events that seemed to confirm that she had no business trusting men, especially strange men who behaved in an odd way, invested too much attention in her too quickly.

Soon she was reliving the time when she'd been running near her college campus at seven o'clock in the morning and a man in an old brown sedan started following her, sending her sprinting through a patch of woods, in desperation to return to campus.

Moments later, she was safe inside her dorm room, the place where she told herself to never go running outside early in the morning, the place where she told herself to never enter a wooded area alone again.

**********

She looked through the front windshield, turned up the volume on the radio and smiled. "I'm okay. I'm okay," she repeated to herself, struggling to calm her nerves, convince herself that she'd make it out of the forest okay.

Gurgling noise in the RV reduced, enough to convince her that she would make it to Bensalem where she had reserved a spot at another campground. Harmony, Soul and Sky, Jennifer Moore, ROSSE and other rhythm and blues hits played on the radio as she made her way out of the state forest.

Then, the gurgling noise grew loud again, unnerving her more than it had the two previous times she'd heard it. Although annoyed, familiarity worked like a trick. While she listened to the hard, choppy noise, she expected the same thing to happen that had happened when she'd heard the noise before, but it didn't.

The RV spun ahead in jerky motions for another five miles, then sputtered. Her two-year-old custom designed, luxury class A RV, with its marble kitchen island, rear bay window and Brazillian cherry wood floors, ran like an old, rusty truck. Seconds later, she lunged forward, her chest pressing into the front panel, when the vehicle came to a sudden halt. Gripping the key, she turned it in the ignition as if doing so would cause the RV to magically restart.

The key had left an imprint on her palm by the time she sat back in the driver's seat and reached for her cellphone. Punching numbers on the phone screen, she dialed 555-1221, then sat back and waited for an RV repair representative to come on the line.

"Hello," she said once she got through to a human technician, shortcutting time she spent answering AI questions. "My RV is stopped on the road in New Jersey. I don't feel safe," she quickly added, looking into the side and rearview mirrors.

The last thing she wanted was to see a van.

"Are you in a public place with other people?"

"No. My RV is completely stopped on a road in the Whooten State Forest."

"Okay. Let's see if we can identify what caused your RV to stop and see if we can't get you up and running again."

"That's what I want," Petula said, surprised to see her hands shaking.

The technician tried to start the RV for several minutes by giving Petula instructions over the telephone while connected to the repair shop via a video cam. Finally, she released an exasperated breath. "I've scheduled an emergency repair technician who will be in a tow truck to come to where you are."

"Thank you. How long will it take for the repair truck to get here?"

"The repairman should be there in half an hour. He's the best repairman to send because he knows the state forest well. We've sent him to Whooten State Forest to help other RVers whose rig broke down. The vehicles rely on electrical and computerized systems. It's probably nothing major. The computer might need to be reset. Happens to new rigs as well as to older rigs."

"If the repairman can get here sooner—"

"--I've scheduled this as an emergency dispatch."

Petula looked through the RV windows and swallowed hard. "Thank you."

She hung up the call and sank down in the driver's seat. The sound of rain tapping the RV pulled her up. As suddenly as it had started to rain, clouds lowered and darkened.

Turning away from the darkening sky, Petula stood and walked back to her bedroom, where she grabbed her gun out of the nightstand. She sat in the driver's seat with the gun on her lap for a long time before she told herself, "This is nuts. I'm being silly."

When she returned to her bedroom, she put the gun back in the nightstand. She'd bought the gun after the incident where she'd run through the woods to safety while she'd been in college. But using the gun was the last thing Petula had hoped to do. As tough and independent as she was, hurting someone was not even a distant wish for her. Hers was a peaceful disposition. A good weekend to her was catching a theater stage play with friends, camping outdoors, visiting a museum or curling up on her back porch swing reading a science fiction novel.

Such a priority was peace and earthiness to her that she'd participated in environmental protection and peace marches while in college and during her early adult years. After she left her parents' home in her late teens, she'd prayed to find a neighborhood with residents that mirrored the global community, intent on connecting with people from a broad range of backgrounds, eager to love and learn from them all. By no means, she knew as she stood in her RV, was she desirous to inflict harm. Yet, and in contrast to her commitment to peace, she told herself that she must protect herself.

While she waited for the tow truck to arrive, she busied herself in the kitchen, making a smoked turkey, goat cheese, lettuce and tomato sandwich, which she washed down with a glass of cold apple juice.

The glass of apple juice was still in her hand when she heard a heavy tapping. Instead of coming from the RV hood or windows, the tapping came from the door.

Halfway to the door, her cellphone rang. "Hello?"

"Is this Petula Abebe?" a woman asked.

"May I ask who's calling?"

"My name is Brenda Larks. I'm the repair center technician you were speaking with about half an hour ago. I dispatched the tow truck repairman to your location."

Petula's eyes lit up. "Oh, yes. Is the repairman here?" Before Brenda answered, she resumed her walk to the front of the RV.

"He should be there in ten minutes."

Petula stopped inches from her RV door. "Are you sure? Can you check to see if he's here now?"

"No. He's not there now. It's standard procedure to call moments before the tow truck technician arrives, so you'll know when to expect them. After he arrives, I'll call you and let you know he's there." After a pause, she added, "It's a safety procedure. But even then, it's good to look at your security cameras and make sure it's the tow truck driver. Once he gets there, I'll stay on the phone with you for a few minutes, and again, it's a safety feature that our company offers its customers."

"Thank you. That's a good feature to have. Will you stay on the line now? Thought I heard somebody knock on the door."

"Sure. I'll hold."

Returning to her bedroom, Petula stood in front of her nightstand, staring at the top drawer. Then, hearing another tap on the front door, she slowly opened the drawer and retrieved her gun then made her way to the front of the RV. Remembering what Brenda had said, she stopped and checked her security console, scanning the RV's entire exterior. She didn't see anyone. When she looked through the windows, she didn't see a van or any other vehicle.

Rain picked up, tapping the RV's hood faster and the sky was darker. If Petula hadn't known better, she would have thought that it was early night instead of mid-afternoon.

"Thanks for holding," she told Brenda. "My mind must be playing tricks on me. Could have sworn that I heard a knock at the door. Checked the security cameras. No one's outside. If you can contact the tow truck driver, can you ask him to put some weight on that truck accelerator? I'm not feeling comfortable out here by myself. It's way too quiet out here for me right now."

"I understand. Let me reach out to him. But just remember, each time I contact him, he has to stop to talk with me."

Her face flushed with rising unease that threatened to turn into outright embarrassment, Petula lowered then raised her head. The sound of her own voice, now jolty with uncertainty, filling with concern about spending the night in the forest in an inoperable vehicle, unnerved her. Swallowing hard and taking in a deep breath, she asked, "Don't you all have hands-free phone capabilities in your vehicles?"

"The tow truck driver might have one. I know they're not in the older tow trucks."

Twisting her shirt collar, Petula said, "If you can check and ask him to drive faster, I'd really appreciate it."

"I will do that. Can I put you on hold?"

"Sure."

Petula tapped her foot on the floor, then she sat on the peach-colored leather sofa and rocked her foot from side-to-side while she waited, one quick rock after another, filling up with distress. Uncertainty poked her, jabbed her like a sharp object, unnerving her; she kept looking at the security console at the front of her RV.

Outside, a growing fog began to blend with the thickening dark. A bump at the back of the RV demanded her attention. She was near the back of the RV when another bump, this one harder than the first, struck the vehicle, a hit that landed with so much force it threw her off balance.

## Chapter Four

Just as Petula leaned forward, looking out of the RV's far back window, a third, much harder bump landed, thrusting her backward. This time she fell, crashing against the floor.

Pulling up by pressing her hands down on her long bedroom dresser, the one across from the foot of her bed, she stared at a man's graying beard. It took her a few seconds to accept that she was looking at Paul.

Her eyes were wide, filled with alarm. Less than twenty yards from her, sitting in his dirty white van, one of his hunting dogs snarling in the front passenger seat next to him, the other dog growling behind him, Paul looked hard at her. He wore a sinister grin. She struggled to make it out, but swore she saw a bow and arrow leaning against the van's interior passenger door.

When she met Paul's stare, she felt hopelessly confused. Try as she might, she could not recall crossing paths with him when she'd lived in Bensalem. They'd not taken the same class in college. She'd never visited the state forest before. Not once had they worked together, and yet he seemed to be following her, determined to bring her misery.

Seeing him smiling the arrogant, lopsided grin filled her with hate. She detested him. If she could have leaped through the window, she would have jumped on him and started swinging wildly, punching him hard in the face. For that she grew angrier, furious at how his presence, his refusal to leave her alone, was changing her, making her want to be unforgiving, mean, hurtful.

Rage was overtaking her. Clenching her fists and gritting her teeth until blood rushed to her face, darkening her cheeks and forehead, she shouted, "Why are you following me?"

Paul's face flattened, going from a grin to a confused expression.

"Why are you following me?" she screamed, shaking her fists at him, spit popping out of her mouth as if lashing out at him. What of the spit didn't land against the back window, deposited in the corners of her mouth.

He grinned, pressed the van's accelerator, and rammed the back of the RV.

"Stop!" Petula yelled, her hands bracing the dresser's edge. She watched his dogs baroo and jump as they locked their gazes on her.

"Stop!"

He rammed his van against the RV. As if he was intent on breaking the RV's rear glass, he repeatedly backed up then rammed the back of the vehicle. He was no longer grinning. His face was contorted, ugly, filled with as much hate and rage as hers.

Mixed in with her hate and rage was rising fear. She wondered if he had done this before, targeting an unassuming woman, stalking the woman for no reason beyond his sick desire to terrorize a woman who didn't know him, someone he could overwhelm and abduct with his size and threatening dogs. The next instant she wondered if he'd stalked a girlfriend or if he'd been married, the perpetrator of domestic violence.

Her refusal to let him assist her while she'd backed her RV into a parking spot when she had first arrived at the forest was simply no reason for his behavior. She had never harmed him, cursed him, or disrespected him.

Ignorance regarding his stalking motive unsettled her, caused her hands to tremor. She turned and looked at the escape door at the side of her bedroom, watching the door rock and shake. Even with the metal of their vehicles separating them, she felt imminent danger.

She saw so much hate in his face, his narrow-focused eyes, his tightly raised shoulders, and his clenched hands, that she was starting to believe that regardless of what she did, even if she pulled a gun on him, he'd get to her and hurt her badly. Her only hope was for the tow truck to arrive.

Glancing at her watch, she begged the tow truck driver to "hurry". It was as if she thought the driver could perform magic and instantly show up, never minding traffic or the ruggedness in the forest's sandy roads.

She stopped clinging to her dresser and tightened her grip on her gun. She held it low, out of Paul's sightline.

Gun in hand, she turned and looked out the back window. Her mouth swung open, forming an "O", giving her space to scream at the top of her lungs.

Paul was gone. Her gaze shifted wildly. Then she ran to the front of the RV, her feet thundering across the floor, her breath thick, as she looked through the windows while she ran.

At the front door, she felt a burst of air then a sharp, stabbing pain. Mixed in with the sharpness, there was heaviness at the center of her back.

Although she tried to turn, she couldn't. She peered at her reflection in one of the long side bay windows, gasping when she saw an arrow fragment, the size of a quarter, stuck in her back. Then, her vision blurred beneath the sharp pain, and she started to feel lightheaded, as if she was about to faint. Blinking frantically, she struggled to take deep breaths, become calm enough to think clearly, but just when she convinced herself that she'd come out of the ordeal alive, her knees buckled.

Jamming her hand inside her front pant pocket, she pulled out her cellphone. She called the RV repair center. "I'm in danger," she said. "A man is trying to kill me. I'm the woman who called you from the Whooten State Forest. My RV is stopped. You were sending a tow truck via an emergency dispatch. Tell them to get here now," she screamed.

Grimacing against the pain, she hung up the phone and dialed 911. "Help! Help! A man is trying to kill me. I'm at the Whooten State Forest. My RV stopped on the sand road headed away from the shore. I was on my way to Bensalem, Pennsylvania. Help! My life is in danger!"

The 911 operator's voice was calm, even. "Who's calling? What is your name?"

"My name is Pe-Petula Ah-Abebe."

"Where did you say you are again?"

"Whooten State Forest."

"Can you get somewhere safe?"

"I'm in my RV, but it won't start."

"Lock your docks and apply all safety features on your RV—"

"—No!" Petula screamed.

It was too late.

Glass at the back of the RV shattered, creating a deafening impact. Paul's dogs leaped through the large breakage in the back window, hurrying toward the front of the RV where Petula stood, the arrow fragment yet in her back.

She grabbed her gun and ran toward the back of the RV, eager to confront Paul. Then her knees shook. Pulling the trigger, she fired two shots at the dogs, barely grazing them.

Seeing the dogs charging toward her, she pulled the trigger again, sending a booming noise through the RV. One of the dogs yelped.

Her hands were shaking when she fired the gun again then yanked on the door separating her bedroom from the front of the RV, trying to close the door. It failed to catch in the lock. Noise from the gun shot blasted in her ears, yet all she saw when she turned was the door being pushed open and the dogs leaping toward her.

The dogs snarling at her heels, she ran to the front of the RV, snatched her keys and shoulder pocketbook, heavier with the cellphone in the front pouch, off the passenger seat, pushed the RV door open, then closed the door, giving herself time to get away from Paul and his dogs.

When she turned, she saw Paul hurrying back to his van. She raced into the woods. She ran for a straight fifteen minutes, zig zagging and tremoring before she ran behind a large tree. Once there, she gritted her teeth and pulled at the arrow fragment. Blood dripped down her back. She kept pulling, but it didn't work. The arrow fragment remained lodged in her back.

Fearing that she would have to use the arrow fragment as a weapon should she run out of ammunition, she leaned against the tree and moved from side to side, squinting and weeping against the searing pain. Blood oozed out of the hole in her back, trickling down her butt and the backs of her legs.

Her hands wet with blood, she stretched her arms until her shoulders ached as she reached for the arrow fragment. She stumbled toward the ground just as she pulled the fragment from her back. Moments later, she stood with greater clarity and balance. "Why?" she mumbled through the haze. "Why are you chasing me?"

In the distance, she heard footsteps. They were faint, far enough away for her to feel like she could make it to the other sand road, a road close to the state forest management office. Nightfall had not yet come, giving her hope.

Inhaling a deep breath, she took off running again, the arrow fragment in one hand and her shoulder pocketbook that held her wallet, gun, cellphone and keys over her shoulder. She staggered and wobbled as she ran, but she dared not stop.

Distant barooing echoed across the forest, alerting her to the growing danger that she was in. She pushed aside low hanging tree limbs as she ran. The scent of water let her know that she was nearing the sand road. It also alerted her to the fact that she was getting closer to Mullic River.

An experienced swimmer, she felt confident that she could swim the deepest parts of the river. Other parts, she was certain she could wade through, even walking along the path next to the river once the dogs had lost her scent. Her only concern was her back, and it gave her great alarm. The last thing that she needed was to suffer another injury or get an infection in her back wound. Her chin shook when she forced herself to accept that fish would pick up the scent of her blood, making her an in-water target.

Barooing grew louder, fierce. She hurried into the river, her legs splashing the water, and submerged herself. Cool waves forced her up out of the water, her nose inches above the surface, her gaze frantically searching the area, landing on rows of trees that stood like tall sentries hiding looming danger. Seconds later, hearing the dogs baroo sent her below the waves, her body engulfed in murky water. Turning away from the shore, she swam far enough underwater to keep the dogs from picking up her scent.

Fish nipped at her back, but she kept swimming. After she had swam three hundred yards, she peered up, barely raising her head above the water, her eyes blinking as the current rolled beneath them.

The dogs were turning. Paul pulled them back, calling them again into the forest.

Petula felt something nipping her legs, but she didn't move. She knew her greatest animal threat in the water was a catfish, trout or largemouth bass biting her, its teeth pulling at her skin, creating small pockets of blood.

Several moments later, she was back on land, running along the path at the river's edge, water dripping off her clothes that clung to her body. Her running led her to an open road, where she stood waving at passing cars and trucks, wondering why she found herself in this dire situation.

Not one driver stopped or slowed down, despite how frantically she waved. Finally, she saw a tow truck ambling down the road, as if the driver was looking for someone.

The driver pulled over, staring at her through the half-lowered driver side window. His voice was gruff, his brunette hair blown-out at the front. "Are you the woman who called the RV repair center about the broken-down class A?"

Petula jogged to the side of the truck, looking over her shoulder for Paul, wondering at his whereabouts, shaken by the fact that she'd become a target of his even as she was completely perturbed as to why he was after her. "Yes. I'm the woman who called the repair center," she nodded, answering the tow truck driver, her voice uneven.

"I saw your RV on the other side of the forest. Not sure why I came this way. Something just told me to drive down this road." He looked at her, noting her wet clothes and disheveled hair. "Hop in. And, by the way; my name is Chris Eggers."

Pulling up on her shoulder pocketbook, she wasted no time climbing inside the truck. When she looked down, she gawked at the dirt and mud clinging to her pants, spotting her hands. "My name is Petula," she told him, rubbing her palms together, working to calm her nerves.

"Do you have the keys to your RV?"

Curling her hands to hide a bit of the dirt and mud, she stammered, "A man is chasing me. I need to get to the nearest police station, or you can take me to a nearby hotel."

He looked at her quizzically, halting in thought for several seconds. Then, glancing at her, he advised, "If someone is chasing you, the best thing to do would be to take you to a police station. You should be safe there." After a pause, he asked, "Do you know the guy?"

Tears pooled in her eyes. She shook her head. "No." A long pause preceded her next words, "I met him while I was at a campground at the state forest."

"Got it," he nodded. Seconds later, he asked, "Why's the guy chasing you?"

While she sat next to Chris, she wondered if there was anything she could have done to stop Paul from fixating on her, from stalking her. She wondered if she should have let him help her back her RV into the parking spot when she'd first arrived at the state forest. Gazing out the tow truck passenger window, she tried to imagine how the situation would be if she'd given into Paul's gesture to help. She wondered if he would have merely helped her park, then left her alone, allowing her to explore the state forest carefree, tucked in safety. But "no" she told herself, accepting that no sane man would stalk her, determined to harm her, simply because she hadn't let him help her park her rig.

Pulling in her bottom lip, she told Chris, "I don't know why Paul's chasing me." She shook her head. "I don't know," she repeated as she rubbed her hand across her forehead. "I found out his name from a couple who had been at the campgrounds before I got there, then they left the next morning. I didn't even have a conversation with the guy. Maybe I remind him of somebody." Her lips quivered. "I don't know. This is all so strange."

"Well, you got out of there; but looks like you took a few hits. Are you okay?" Placing his hand on her shoulder, he pushed her forward. "Are you bleeding?"

She sat back, grimacing against the pain. "I'll need to get to a doctor, but first I want to get to the police. I called the police before the guy forced me out of my RV."

"Let me call in the pickup and let them know you're in danger." A moment later, he hung up his cellphone and nodded at her while he pulled away from the side of the road and drove toward the nearest exit. "The RV repair center knows I picked you up. Now, let's get you some help."

For the next hour, they rode in silence. Then, he turned onto a city highway, leaving the state forest.

She listened to the Bruce Ruskin song playing on the radio. "I'm so glad you showed up when you did."

"RVing is a lot of fun, a great way to see the world. But there are risks. Seems like you were prepared. A lot of people might not have made it out like you did. Sounds like that guy who was chasing you has some serious mental health issues."

"For sure."

"No reason to attack someone, especially somebody you don't know."

Rain drummed the hood of the tow truck when they pulled into the parking lot of a smalltown police station, a one-story dull beige brick building. Four police cruisers were parked at the front of the building. Half a dozen civilian vehicles, four SUVs and two electric cars, sprinkled the rest of the parking lot.

Petula gripped her pocketbook strap then opened the passenger door. "Will you please wait until I come out of the police station?"

"Sure."

She climbed out of the tow truck and started walking toward the police station. "Thank you so much."

Chris rolled the window down. "Want me to come with you?"

She stopped walking. "Please."

Together they walked into the police station, a building no bigger than a small office with four back rooms where locals engaged in criminal activity were processed and suspects were interviewed.

They weren't in the police station for long, the officers Petula talked to seemed bored, as if they couldn't wait to get home. "We'll be on the lookout for this Paul guy," they told her, glancing at the tow truck driver.

Chris and she stood.

"Thank you," she told the officers, certain that she'd never hear from them again.

Soon Chris and she were outside in the parking lot. "Where are you from?"

"Outside of Atlanta, but that's not important." She shrugged. "Why's that matter?"

"Do you know anyone around here?"

"I have friends in Bensalem."

"Let me take you to your friends or take you somewhere safe and wait for your friends to come and get you."

She peered at the sky before she looked at him. "Do you think it would be safe to go back and see if we can get my RV started?"

"Honestly, with the weather," he said peering at the sky, "I think it would be best to wait until morning to go back and try to start your RV."

She twisted her mouth, nibbled her bottom lip then nodded. "You're probably right."

"I know you didn't ask for this and I'm not trying to make a pass at you or anything, but I live about fifteen miles from here. Do you know where the historic Patricia B. Hart house is outside of Doylestown?"

"Oh, yeah. I do," Petula said, happy to shift her thoughts away from Paul and the danger she found herself in. She almost smiled, eager to forget her troubles, to pretend that she hadn't been chased, forced to flee the campgrounds. "My nephew, Gregory, and I visited the house two years ago." She smiled. "I love to write and read science fiction and literary novels. We both enjoyed visiting the house. After the visit to the author's childhood home, I started reading Patricia B. Hart's novels and enjoyed them. She was a talented writer."

"I'm not much of a book reader, but a lot of people visit that house each year. I don't live far from there."

"I appreciate you kinda offering to let me stay at your place, but I don't want to impose. Is there a hotel in the area where I can stay? If so, I'll just stay there for the night. Is there a way you can tow my RV tomorrow if I give you the keys? You know where the RV is."

"Sure. I'll call it in and take another guy out there with me."

They returned to the tow truck and pulled out of the police station parking lot onto the road. Ten minutes passed when Petula saw a hotel. "We can pull in there," she pointed.

As Chris drove toward the hotel parking lot, Petula spotted a dirty white van on the other side of the road, moving in the opposite direction, the driver scanning one side of the road, then the other.

She scrunched down in the passenger seat.

Chris peered at her. "See someone?"

"I think the guy who was chasing me is in that van."

Chris looked over his shoulder, spotting the van. "Looks like there are two dogs in that van."

When the van circled back around, nearing the hotel, Chris looked at her, worry on his face. "The offer to stay with me at my place for the night still stands. You'll be safe there. Promise I won't bother you. If you want, I can even have my two little brothers stay the night. They are nine and eleven years old. And I can clean that wound in your back and patch it up at my place. That or I can take you to the hospital or you can go back to the police station."

"Going back to the police station might be best," she said. "But that station is so small." Peering at Chris she asked, "Does it stay open all night?"

Chris shrugged, "Not sure." Raising his cellphone, he searched for the police station. After he found the station's website, he dialed the number and pressed the speaker button on his phone. "What time is your waiting room open to the public?" he asked after a clerk at the station answered.

"Eight o'clock," the clerk answered. Seconds later, the clerk asked, "Why?"

"Wanted to know a place someone could stay at safely for the night."

"Have them come in, but we close to the public at eight o'clock. There'll be a dispatcher here, but that's it. No one can just sit here all night."

"Thank you," Chris said, glancing at Petula.

Petula looked over her shoulder at the van, wishing that it didn't exist. Biting down on her bottom lip, she wrestled with the idea of staying at Chris' home, staying with any man. The pain of injuries she'd suffered from men lingered, the same way that the pain in her back remained dull at times, sharp at other times, depending on the way that she moved her body.

For years, she had wished that she could forgive the men who had hurt her so she could go free. Yet, something held her back, caused her to trust no man, to suspect every man of wanting to harm her.

Now, she was at a crossroads. She could either have him drive her to a hospital and hope Paul didn't follow her there, reserve a room at a hotel in this strange town where people might know and trust Paul or she could go with Chris, a man who had, up until now, only been helpful to her.

She sighed and stared across the road. It surprised her when she saw the van parked across the street from the hotel. "I'll go with you, but only for a little while. I'm sure Paul will clear out of the area soon and go back to the campground." Seconds later, she looked at Chris and asked, "Are you sure we'll be safe?" Staring at her cellphone and clenching her jaw, she wished that she'd stayed in Atlanta until her friends Gloria and James had arrived home.

Chris nodded. "I'm sure we'll be safe. If it comes to it, I'll call some friends and have them lookout for us."

"You're really a good dude?"

He laughed. "I'm a former Navy seal. I know how to handle myself and I've never hurt anyone outside of serving in the military, nor do I want to."

She sighed. "Okay." She knew she didn't have many other options, at least not now. She prayed to God that she was making the right choice.

Chapter Five

Rain and fog blended, creating a haze across the town, hinting at twilight, by the time Chris drove the tow truck up the long gravel driveway at the side of his sky blue and white ranch home. While he drove, he glanced at Petula, taking note of her perceptions of the house.

Although the ranch house sat on two acres of land, it was a modest dwelling. Petula sat close to the passenger door looking through the window, watching bits of gravel pop as the truck continued up the driveway. The front yard was open, wide, reminding Petula of her maternal great-grandmother's property, a place Ariana and she visited infrequently, their mother walking toward the middle front of them, when they were in elementary school.

She turned away from the window when she saw two bull terriers race towards Chris after he put the tow truck in park. The dogs leaped up, their front paws scratching the driver's door, tails wagging.

Petula leaned against the passenger door, becoming suddenly leery. "Is this your tow truck?"

"No. The tow truck belongs to the repair shop, but they checked it out to me when they hired me. Don't worry," he chuckled. "I don't take advantage of it. The guy

I replaced quit because he was on call so much, driving to the strangest out-in-the-middle-of-nowhere places during the day and night to help people stranded in their RV." Looking at her, he added, "In other words, being able to keep the tow truck at home isn't all upsides."

"Do you think you'll have to go on call tonight?"

He shrugged. "Don't know."

"I can't stay out here by myself."

He looked at her, smiling faintly. "Don't worry. I'll take you with me if I get a call."

She twisted her mouth. "When are you going to pick up your two younger brothers?"

"As soon as I lock you in the cellar," he said, bursting out laughing.

She watched the dogs jump up on the driver's side door. Chris' attempt at humor about the cellar unnerved her. She ran her hands down the front of her shirt, the image of the Atlanta Buckhead skyline stretching long when she pulled on the shirt's hem. As soon as she looked down and saw her fingers tremor, she shoved her hands inside her lap.

"You have trouble trusting people, don't you?"

"I've had my share of unfortunate experiences, especially with men."

"I would never lock you or anyone in a cellar. I don't even have a cellar. I can tell you jump to negative conclusions."

"Don't mean to. It's a habit." She looked at the dogs. "Are your dogs friendly?"

"They are with me," he smiled. "But you don't have to worry. Regardless of how they are with you as someone new to them, I won't let them hurt you. I don't want to see you hurt period, which is why you're in this tow truck right now. I could have just drove right by you back at the state forest."

She worked at a grin but only managed to twist her mouth. "But you wouldn't do that."

"You're right. I wouldn't." Placing his hand on the doorknob, he asked her, "Ready?"

"Can you put your dogs up first?" Petula asked, images of Paul's dogs fresh in her memory.

"Tell you what. I'll walk over to your side of the truck and walk to the house with you. I doubt the dogs will bother you. I won't let them jump up on you and when they see me walking next to you, they'll view you as a friend."

"That's the thing I do like about dogs," she said. "They see the human who feeds them as the alpha dog."

"Yep. That's why dogs are so loyal, especially if you play with them and are kind to them."

As soon as he stepped out of the tow truck, the dogs started jumping up on him, their mouths open as if they were smiling as they looked up at him. "Get down," he told the dogs when he reached the passenger door.

Petula was reluctant to exit the truck, but she did, slowly sliding off the seat and standing close to Chris. She took small steps while she walked next to him, her gaze fixed on the dogs who walked on Chris' right side. Then, seeing that the dogs weren't going to harm her, she opened her stride and started walking at a normal pace.

"You've got a nice ranch house," was the first thing she said when Chris unlocked the door and stepped to the side so she could enter his home. "Roomy leather sofa," she continued, surveying the living room. "Who arranged the live flowers and who hung those paintings on the walls?" She couldn't stop examining the house, taking in the original paintings hanging on the walls, pieces of unique artwork on the end tables and the expansive kitchen, a marble island at its center. "Do you live here alone?"

"Yes. I live here alone, and I decorated the place."

"You have a strong artistic eye."

A smile was on his face when he left the living room, where Petula continued to stand, and entered the kitchen. "I'm an artist."

He was carrying a box of gauze pads and a bottle of antiseptic when he returned to the living room. "Sit in this chair," he told Petula, pointing his head toward a brown chair. "I'm going to clean your back wound and apply a sterile gauze pad."

Petula sat still, leaning forward, for less than five minutes. "That was fast," she said when she stood, holding the box of gauze pads Chris gave her before he reentered the kitchen.

The dogs in the kitchen with Chris, lapping water out of their bowls that were pushed against a wall next to the steps that led into the finished basement, Petula relaxed. Her shoulders even lowered. She stepped close to the paintings and looked up at them. "Did you paint these?"

"Sure did."

When she looked toward the kitchen, she saw him leaning against the archway.

He took a bite out of a peanut butter and jelly sandwich. "Want one?" he asked, holding the sandwich out to her.

"No, thanks," she told him. "Do you have orange or apple juice or even a bottle of kombucha?"

"Let's see," he told her after he stuck his head in the refrigerator. "One peach flavored kombucha coming up," he said, handing her a cold bottle of the beverage.

"I started drinking kombucha when I stopped drinking soda. Wanted something with a kick, but less sugar."

"Kombucha does have a little kick—" Refrigerator door closed, he froze. The kitchen light flickered and, facing the living room, Chris stared at the door.

As if following his direction, Petula's body stiffened, but not before she turned away from him, searching for what had demanded his attention.

The dogs hurried to the center of the kitchen floor; their ears were erect.

"Did you hear that noise?" Petula asked. "Sounded like someone was on your porch."

This time when she turned, Chris was gone. So were the dogs. Turning in a circle, she wondered where they had gone and so fast.

"Chris?"

"Ssshhh," he said, stepping back into the kitchen with the dogs on his heels.

"Where did you go?"

"Into the basement," he told her, raising a steel baseball bat.

"Do you think it's your brothers on the porch?"

"No. I haven't called my mom yet to ask her if she wants to drop them off or have me pick them up and," he added, rolling his eyes, "I wouldn't get a bat if I thought it was them."

She followed him and the dogs out of the kitchen, through the living room to the edge of the front door. Once at the living room's edge, she went to the window and peered through the blinds.

While she peered through the blinds, Chris squinted and looked through the peep hole in the door. "Don't say anything. Just nod," he whispered to Petula as he watched the man on the porch. "Is that the guy from the van? I didn't get a good look at him before when we might have seen him over by the hotel, but you've seen him. Is that him?"

She squinted and looked through a slight opening in the blinds. "Yes. That's him. I'll never forget that man. I didn't do anything to him," she stammered. "And he just came after me for no reason at all."

"Okay. Okay," he whispered, pushing his hand down again and again, eager for her to silence. "We can't let him hear us, although he's bound to know we're in here. That's the only reason he's here."

Releasing the blinds and stepping back, she looked at Chris who continued to look through the peep hole. "How would he know where you live?"

He shrugged. He didn't move away from looking through the peep hole, watching every move Paul made.

She approached Chris. When she did, the dogs turned from watching the door to watching her. "You've never seen him before?"

"No."

She dropped her shoulders and lowered her head, then she raised her head again. "I apologize. Didn't mean to bring any trouble into your life. Don't want any trouble in my life either." She sighed. "It's like he's a ghost. Somehow, he knows where to find me. He keeps knowing just where to go and when." Shaking her head, she said, "It's too uncanny for me. I'm not accustomed to this."

Chris frowned. "I'm not accustomed to this either."

"I'm not saying you are—"

"—I'm as confused about this as you are." He turned away from her in a half circle then faced her again. "You've been treating me like I'm some bad guy since we pulled up to my place. I'm not going to hurt you," he added, raising his voice. "I don't want you, me or anyone to be stalked or feeling unsafe." Releasing a deep breath, he told her, "Just trying to help you. Like you probably feel with that guy out front, I'm starting to feel like I got pulled into this."

She paused, then asked, "What do you think it was like for me out there in the forest all by myself with that guy banging his van into the back of my stalled-out RV? For all I know, he did something to cause my RV to start running ragged and then stop. What do you think that was like, being out in the forest by myself like that? Talk about scared. I was scared out of my wits."

"Trust me. I don't know who that guy is, never seen him before."

Chris suddenly stopped talking. When he looked at the door, he pulled on his dogs' collars and started moving backwards.

Petula didn't follow Chris, not this time. Instead, she peered through the blinds. Seeing an empty porch, she turned and looked at Chris who had moved back to the kitchen, his hands still on the dogs' collars. He was leaning forward as if he was waiting for something.

"Where did he go?" she whispered. She looked all the way to one end of the porch then all the way to the other end. There was no one on the porch. There was no one in the yard. She didn't even see a van.

"What are you doing all the way over by the kitchen?" she asked Chris, her back now to the window. A second later, she heard a loud banging noise. It sounded like someone had plunged a metal crane against the front of the house.

By the time she turned, the front door was rocking on its hinges.

She ran backwards, out of harm's way. Then, just as quickly, she ran toward the window again.

Chris raced inside the kitchen to the top of the basement stairwell. He sprinted back inside the living room carrying a blast launcher rifle. Unlocking then yanking the front door open, he fired several rounds of the rifle at the front of Paul's van, puncturing the windshield.

This time when Petula looked outside, she saw Paul, his head lying across the van's steering wheel.

She hurried to the door. "What did you do?" she stammered, her hand clutching her chest, fearful that she'd somehow brought trouble to Chris' home because of Paul. "Did you kill him?" Her shoulders tremored. "I can't-I can't deal with this—" She screamed, "I don't even know this guy. I don't know why he's following me, but I don't want to murder him."

Pulling her away from the entrance, Chris closed the door. "I shot him with non-lethal blasts pellets." Shaking his head, he continued, "I don't want to kill anyone any more than you do, but it's a crazy world. Gotta have a way to fend for myself." His head pointed toward the rifle. "That's why I have a non-lethal weapon." Facing the doorway again, he said, "He shouldn't be out long. Leave the door closed."

Her gaze darted while she was also relieved that she hadn't just become witness to a murder. She blurted, "But he's knocked out. This is the best time to subdue him, find a way to keep him inside the van, and make sure he doesn't come after us again."

Chris stormed across the floor toward her. "Keep the door closed," he shouted, jabbing his finger against his chest. Raising his hands, as if surrendering, he added, "You definitely shouldn't go out there." He made clear. "He's not after me. He's after you."

She looked at him with a blank stare. "No. This time he was after both of us. This is your house. From the looks of it," she said peering through the blinds at the van, "he was going to drive that van right through your front door."

"Even so, leave the door closed. I've called the police."

Absent another word, she tightened her grip on the doorknob and yanked the door open.

Paul was rolling his head, starting to lift it off the steering wheel. She didn't see his basenjs next to or behind him and wondered if they had suffered serious injuries.

At the same time, Chris' bull terriers came to the front door then stepped onto the porch, eyeing the van. Petula watched them point their noses in the air and sniff hard, as if trying to make out the scent of Paul's dogs, ready to attack.

Chris grabbed Petula's arm, squeezing her skin until it pinched. "Get back in the house," he hollered, jerking on her arm.

Petula shook free of Chris' clenching grasp. "It's time I confronted him. I have a right to know why he's after me," she screamed, the shrill in her voice going out across the yard.

Running to the edge of the porch, Chris snatched her forearm and pulled her toward the door. "What if he has a lethal gun?"

Lifting her shoulder bag against her chest, she said, "There isn't an arrow in my back and I'm not alone." She fastened her gaze on Paul, not flinching, the weight of her gun now in her hand. "This time I'm ready."

Chapter Six

While Paul shook his head, moving further into consciousness, a white and gray police cruiser pulled up in the driveway, the car's siren spinning, lights flashing. Petula released a breath when she saw that the police officer wasn't one of the officers that Chris and she had spoken with earlier at the police station.

"Just what is the problem?" the officer began after he exited the cruiser, his bodycam activated, his hand on his holster.

Petula hurried toward the officer, "This man ran his van into my RV at the Whooten State Forest, then he shows up here, trying to get in this man's house," she screamed.

The officer raised his hand. "Stay there," he told Petula. His hand on his holster, the officer approached the van carefully. "Hey," he called as he knocked on the van's driver door with the end of his flashlight. "Place both of your hands on the steering wheel."

Petula fixed her gaze on the van. It startled her when she felt her shoulders open then lower, signaling her growing hope that the ordeal with Paul was over. She watched Paul with an intensity she hadn't felt in years. She hated thinking that he could hold her future in his hands.

If he didn't stop stalking her, chasing her for reasons yet unknown to her, she would never feel completely free, she told herself. Should he fulfill her request to leave her alone, not once again encounter her however long either of them remained in the county or anywhere else in the world, she knew she would feel liberated, safe, in the clear, but only if he left her alone. Shaking her head didn't dissipate the feeling; it thickened in her mouth like a bitter bile substance. She hated that Paul, a strange man, had become an axle in her life.

Several tense seconds passed before Paul placed his hands on the steering wheel. Almost as soon as he did, his hands started to slip into his lap and his head bobbed and weaved.

"Keep both your hands on the steering wheel," the police officer demanded, his voice stern.

Paul's hands again on the steering wheel, the officer opened the driver's door. "Step out of the vehicle slowly. Raise your hands while you exit."

Gradually, Paul exited the van, his hands high in the air. "I must have fainted," he told the officer. Shaking his head, he added, "I don't know what happened. I must have passed out." He wobbled toward the officer.

"Stop," the officer ordered. "Stay right there. Move slowly and get your driver's license and registration."

License and registration in hand, the officer told Paul, "I'm going to cuff you for everyone's safety, then I'm going to run your tags."

While the officer stepped to the back of the van, Paul stood frozen with his cuffed hands behind his back. As faint as he'd made out to be, he found enough energy to stare at Petula.

She held his glare. She wanted nothing more than to let him know that she was not going to be led by fear; she was not going to license him to control her in any way. She knew how to stand up, and that's exactly what she was going to do. Even as she stared back at him, she still wanted to get an answer to the question that she'd asked him back at the campgrounds. She wanted to know why he was pursuing her. And so, the officer present, she stepped off the porch, approached Paul and asked him point blank, "Why are you doing this to me?"

The officer looked at her. "Don't engage in conversation." Lifting his car phone, he called in the license and registration. Moments later, he returned Paul the identification. Looking at Petula, he asked Paul, "How do you know her? What's your relationship to the young lady?"

Paul grinned at Petula while he said, "We've been having some disagreements lately."

"I don't know him," Petula snapped, her brow tight, one of her hands formed into a fist. "I've never seen this man before," she shouted.

Paul looked hard at Petula. "You know that's not true."

"That one time—" Petula tried, frowning at the memory of early encounters with Paul at the state forest.

"--Just a moment," the officer ordered Petula. His gaze shifted to Chris, who stood at the edge of the bottom porch step, less than five yards from Petula. The officer pulled out his notepad and a pen. "What's your involvement in this?"

"I'm a RV repairman. Her RV was broken down. She phoned it into the repair center, and I was dispatched to the Whooten State Forest to try to help her get her RV started. If I couldn't get the RV started, I was directed to tow the vehicle to our nearest repair center which is about ten miles from here and over forty miles from the state forest."

Turning from Petula and Paul, the officer asked Chris, "So, you never saw or spoke with the young lady before you went out to try to start her RV?"

"That's correct."

Tilting his head toward Paul, the officer asked Chris, "Was he there when you got to the state forest and the place where her RV was broken down?"

"No. He wasn't there," Chris said. "We didn't see him until after we stopped by the police station then drove to a hotel."

The officer stopped writing on his notepad. "Did I ask you for all that information?"

Chris gawked at the officer.

"I've got to keep the facts straight. Only answer what I ask you."

Petula rolled her eyes. "Arrest him," she shouted, pointing at Paul, rage building within her.

"Ma'am," the officer said, looking at Petula. "I need you to be quiet while I get some background information on what's going on here."

Petula stepped back and clenched her teeth.

"What time did you go to the police station and which station did you go to?" the officer asked Chris.

Clearing her throat, Petula said, "We went to the police station around three o'clock. This all happened today."

The officer pursed his lips and flipped the end of his pen toward Chris. "I was talking to him."

Chris glanced at Petula then focused his attention on the officer. "What she said is accurate. And we went to the police station on Wellington Street."

"Is this your house?" the officer asked Petula.

"No. It's his house," she answered, tilting her head toward Chris. "He was nice enough to offer me a place to stay seeing as I was damn near stranded on foot when we crossed paths, but I'm going to stay at a hotel."

Looking from Petula to Chris to Paul, the officer nodded, "I think that's a good idea. Do you have a way to get to a hotel?"

Petula shook her head, "No."

The officer looked at Chris. "Do you remember who you spoke with at the station?"

Chris shook his head. "No. I don't."

"Do you?" the officer asked, turning toward Petula.

"No."

"But the officers you spoke with made a report?"

"They were taking notes," Chris told him.

"Then, they made a report," the officer nodded. "That's good." Looking at Petula, he said, "You always want a paper trail, especially when dealing with characters like this guy," he added, nodding toward Paul.

Petula's shoulders rose and stiffened as she followed the officer's gaze and looked at Paul. She stood bold and tall; yet her widening eyes betrayed her efforts at bravery, hinting at the fear that she felt.

Glancing at her, the officer asked, "Do you feel safe?"

"No." She scowled at Paul. "I don't even know him."

"If that's what you want to say," Paul said. "But you know we know each other."

"No, we don't," Petula shouted, looking from the officer to Chris to Paul, suddenly worried that the officer might mistake the situation as a domestic dispute. "Ask him why he's following me and why he rammed his van into the back of my RV and why he's trying to hurt me?"

"Answer her question," the officer instructed.

Paul shrugged. He smiled at Petula then quickly looked away from her, wearing a bashful grin. A gust of wind blew over his dirty blonde hair that was neatly brushed back, away from his forehead — smooth as silk, the bandana nowhere in sight. A blistering bruise the size of the bottom of a soda bottle crowned the top right corner of his temple, result of his head having banged against his van's steering wheel when he'd fallen unconscious after Chris had fired the non-lethal pellets at him.

Rubbing his fingers together, Paul smiled at Petula, as if beckoning her.

It surprised Petula how clean Paul's hands were. Even his fingernails were clean, neatly trimmed, their ends low and round. Except for the beard, his face was smooth. If he hadn't accosted her or opened his mouth, revealing his cracked, stained teeth, or driven a dirty white van, Petula would have sworn that he was a successful financier, chemist or perhaps an established surgeon. No longer interested in his hands, she looked at his square shoulders and his piercing blue eyes. After she took in the scent of a faint cologne that pushed off his body when a slight wind blew, she turned away from him.

"To answer your question, Officer," Paul said, turning from Petula to the cop, his tone confident, "I offered to help her back her RV in without it getting scratched up when she first arrived at the campgrounds."

"The campgrounds at the Whooten State Forest?" the officer asked for clarity.

Paul nodded. "Yes."

Petula fixed her gaze on the officer. She refused to give Paul any more of her attention. "I've backed my RV up on my own many times. I told him that I didn't need help. He seemed offended. Why, I don't know, as I had never, even once in my life, seen him before." Gritting her teeth, she said, "Wonder if he's previously done that to another woman. Wonder if he's stalked and tried to hurt another woman before." She stared at Paul's pant pockets, searching for the Custom Accounting Designs keychain, but it was not to be found.

The officer glanced at Paul.

"I was ju-just trying to be nice," Paul stammered. "I was just trying to be helpful."

"It doesn't matter if you two know each other or not, when someone asks you to leave them alone, that's what you do," the officer told him.

"Got it," Paul nodded.

"Now, that we hopefully have that cleared up. What are you doing in this man's yard, nearly up on his porch?"

"Like I said earlier, I must have passed out—"

The officer twisted his mouth. "—And ended up in this man's front yard?"

"I-I-I must have taken a wrong turn. I didn't mean anyone any harm."

Pulling up on his belt, the officer asked, "Where were you headed? Where were you trying to be?"

Shrugging and looking at the ground, then into his van at his dogs who were now looking out the back window, Paul stuttered, "I wa-was just out taking a drive, just out driving."

"Just out driving and you suddenly passed out?" the officer asked, his brow raised. He examined Paul, his wide eyes, stout frame, and sullen expression. Then, he turned away from Paul and called for backup and for a tow truck.

No longer on his radio, he returned his attention to Paul. "Let's do an intoxication test, shall we?"

At the request, Paul stood taller, shoulders back, showcasing his six-foot, four-inch frame. His stride was open, his long legs closing the gap that separated the police officer and him.

Petula and Chris stood in silence while the officer gave Paul the test. Their mouths turned down when they heard the officer's next words.

"You haven't been drinking," the officer said at the end of the test, again pulling up on his belt. "I want you to tell me exactly why you're in this man's yard. This time, tell the truth."

"Okay," Paul sighed. "I wanted to see if we could mend our relationship."

The officer looked at Petula, awaiting a response.

"I don't know him at all. There is no relationship to mend, and I want to know why he rammed the back of my RV with his van?"

The officer turned toward Paul.

Paul shrugged. He eyeballed the officer blankly, coldly. "My emotions got the best of me. I got out of hand. When I love someone, I love them fully—" He stopped, realizing that he'd said too much.

"I'm ordering you to stay away from her," the officer snapped. "Do you understand?"

"Yes. Yes, Sir."

"That means you don't end up anywhere else she is. Understand?"

"Yes, Sir."

"Even if you faint or get lost, you don't end up in a yard, a hotel, anywhere that she is. Understand?"

"Yes, Sir."

His notepad closed and shoved in his pant pocket, the officer asked Petula, "Would you like to file a criminal harassment report for stalking?"

"Yes."

"Would you also like to request a restraining order be placed on Paul Gibbs?"

Paul's eyes widened when the officer revealed his surname.

"Yes. I would like to file a criminal harassment report for stalking against him and request a restraining order?" In her mind, she kept repeating Paul's surname to herself, "Gibbs. Gibbs. Gibbs." She made a note to do a search on Paul Gibbs when she got to a safe place. A surname -- to her it was another piece of information with which to identify Paul and potentially discover his past indiscretions, find out if he had stalked other women. If she got his license plate number, she knew she could find out where he lived.

Seeing another police cruiser, followed by a tow truck, speeding up the gravel driveway, the officer broke up her thoughts. "Okay. We can create a criminal harassment report now. You'll have to file a restraining order with the clerk of the court."

"Thank you."

"Here's my card. If you need help again, just dial 911," the officer said as he leaned toward her. Looking up at Chris, he said, "That goes for you too."

Chris nodded. "Thanks."

Turning to Petula, the officer said, "You can come with me down to the station if you'd like." Looking toward the recently arrived cop, he told Paul, "You're going with him. Your vehicle will be towed to the station."

"Yes, Sir," Paul nodded, nearly bowing in feigned submission, as if he was merely acknowledging a member of the Royal family.

The officer looked toward the porch at Chris. "You know that you can file an incident report against him for the damages he caused to your property, right?"

"Yes," Chris said.

"Would you like to do that?"

"Sure." Chris shrugged. "But it's not that bad, a few porch floorboards loosened."

Petula looked at Chris with a growing curiosity. In a warm and welcoming way, he was odd to her. Since he'd picked her up at the state forest, his had been a calming nature. Not only had he offered to help her as soon as she climbed inside his truck, but he'd also been patient, driving her to the police station and even offering to take her to a hotel before they arrived at his ranch house. And when his home had been threatened with Paul charging the front steps with his van, rather than grabbing a pistol, Chris had run for a bat and later a non-lethal gun. To Petula, Chris was intent on causing no harm, even if vengeance seemed warranted.

The officer walked across the yard, moving between Petula and Chris. Handing Chris the incident report, he said, "You never know how bad the damages are at first glance. Recommend that you contact your insurance company tonight or first thing in the morning to file for damages."

A few feet away, Paul smirked at Chris, his lips going up in a clown-like smile.

When the officer looked at Petula, he followed her stare as she examined Chris' and Paul's body language, their slouching shoulders and relaxed hips, how they eyeballed each other.

Breaking Petula's concentration, the officer asked, "Do you two know each other?"

Chris was slow to answer. "No," he finally said, looking at Paul more than he looked at the officer.

The officer turned to Paul.

"Never seen him before." He waited for the officer to turn away from him, then he looked toward the porch and smiled at Chris.

Petula shuddered when she saw Paul smile at Chris, feeling betrayed. *"And to think I was going to stay at Chris' house,"* she thought, distrust building inside her. It concerned her that not once had she seen Chris do or say anything off putting while she'd been in his tow truck. *"Fear of Paul made me trust Chris,"* she scowled. *"How could I have ever been willing to stay at a strange man's house?"* She looked toward the sky, stars lighting up the night like diamonds, and rolled her eyes.

"Not sure I believe either of you," the officer said, breaking up Petula's train of thought as he looked from Chris to Paul. "Come with me," he told Petula.

She followed the officer to the cruiser, where she filed a criminal harassment report for stalking against Paul. While the officer wrote out the incident report, she looked at Paul and Chris, eager to spot a hint that they were in this together.

After the report was filed, the officer gave her a copy of the report. Her hands were trembling when she took hold of the report.

The officer glanced at her hands, then told her. "I can take you back to the station."

Her face tightened as, emotion rising within her, she fought back tears. "I really need to get my RV, and I need to get it running again."

The officer smiled. "Don't worry." Stepping away from her, he updated the second cop on the situation. Then, the second officer directed Paul to the back seat of his cruiser while the tow truck driver hitched up Paul's van, dogs barooing inside. Moments later, both the second cruiser and tow truck had turned and driven back down the driveway toward the street.

Again at Petula's side, the first officer assured her that, "There are a few RV repair shops you can go to. You'll get your RV fixed. We can even call a repair shop from the police station."

"There probably isn't a repair shop open at this hour."

"Do you have a 24-hour roadside assistance package?"

She nodded, "I do."

"Then, you can find a place to take your vehicle."

"But my roadside assistance number has limited repair shop options."

"I'm telling you, there's bound to be an emergency RV roadside assistance company that you can get help from. Doylestown is small, but you can get help even at this hour."

"Okay."

"Do you have money for a hotel?"

"I do, but I can't stay anywhere that Paul can find me." Seconds later, she asked, "Will Paul be kept overnight?"

"He'll be booked. If he has a good attorney and the judge is lenient, he could be released tonight, especially considering that I don't think Chris is going to press charges and it doesn't look like Paul struck you or Chris," he told her. "Do you have family or friends in the area?"

"I have friends in Bensalem."

"Bensalem isn't far from here. Call your friends from the station. I'm sure they'll come to get you. This might be easier to solve than you think."

"Okay. Let me just tell Chris that I'm going to the station."

He smiled faintly at her. "Sure."

"Thank you for picking me up at the state forest," Petula began, her hands cupped and turned palms upward, as she approached Chris. Her thoughts volleying back to her RV, she leaned toward him and said, "I hate to ask you for anything else. But," she began, her gaze turning upward, observing the night sky. In an instant, she marveled at the growing darkness, the hint of rain amid what, to her, felt like an unstable calm. Then, just as quickly as she'd surveyed the sky, she returned her attention to Chris, studying his smooth forehead and his gentle smile, not a hint of anger or frustration on his face. She wondered if Chris buried hard emotions that arose from within him. She wondered if he saw himself as a servant of sorts, a man who did what it took to ensure those who sought his support were safe.

"Tomorrow will you please go get my RV and tow it to a repair shop close to Bensalem?" She scanned his face. "I've got to get my RV running again."

"Sure," he nodded. "If the call comes through to me, I'll pick up your tow truck. Just call the repair center tomorrow morning and request the tow." He looked at her. "Employees must keep a trail of pick-ups and repair center drop-offs which is why you need to call it in tomorrow, but I can pick it up. I remember where your RV is. If it's not me," he assured her, "whoever gets the call, will get your rig towed to a good local repair shop."

His honesty disarmed her earlier misgivings about him however slight they were. "Thank you for everything," she said, raising the box of gauze pads, smiling and backing away from him.

## Chapter Seven

Night was descending hard on the town, cloaking it in a thickening darkness. Petula told herself that she had to go with the officer, although he had never verbally shared his name. When he returned to her side, she searched his chest for a badge. Thankful that hers was an excellent memory, she made note of the badge number. Then, she turned over the business card he'd given her and took note of his name, Officer Monroe Duggan.

She climbed inside the back seat of the cruiser while Officer Duggan climbed behind the wheel of the car. Before they backed out of the driveway, she rolled the window down and told Chris, "Thank you."

The ride was quiet, Officer Duggan watching the road while Petula sat in the back seat wondering how she got in the situation she found herself in, feeling trapped, bound to her current predicament.

The first thing she did when they got to the station was to ask where the clerk of the court office was so she could file a restraining order against Paul. Then, she went into the waiting area and called Gloria and James. She knew they weren't home, as they weren't supposed to get together for another few days but hope and desperation demanded that she push that fact aside.

Guilt stabbed her thoughts. She didn't want to worry her friends, causing them to rush back home just because she had made a bad decision and gone to an unfamiliar outdoor area alone.

It took deep nerve, but she did dial Gloria's cellphone number. The phone rang five times then switched to voice mail.

"Hey, Gloria. This is Petula. Girl, you won't believe what happened to me. I don't want to get you alarmed, but I'm sitting at the South Doyle police station. Some guy was following me, started when I was at the Whooten State Forest campgrounds. Remember I told you I was going there before we met up? Anyhow, call me when you get this message. I know you're in Orlando. Just wanted to talk."

At the same time Petula heard the voice mail click off, the sound of approaching footsteps demanded her attention. When she looked up, she was surprised to see Officer Duggan, as moments ago she'd last seen him leaning over a counter in the station's rear administrative area.

He sipped hot, black coffee from a paper cup. "Is your friend Gloria coming to get you?"

Rather than answer him, Petula sat back in the chair and wondered how he knew her friend's name was Gloria. She hadn't seen him while she'd been leaving the voice mail message.

"Yes. Yes, she is. She's coming." She stood. "Thank you for your help."

"Be careful," Officer Duggan called out to her moving back as he watched her exit the police station.

On her way out of the police station, Petula wondered if she should contact an Uber driver and just go to Bensalem tonight. By the time she'd stepped outside, she'd made up her mind.

She was leaning against the police station's brick exterior when she pulled out her cellphone and requested an Uber driver, far enough away from the door to prevent Officer Duggan from seeing her.

Light rain started tapping her shoulders and feet. Despite the weather, she remained outside. Then minutes later, the Uber driver pulled into the station parking lot.

She hurried inside the back of the car.

The Uber driver glanced into the rearview mirror. "You're going to the Mango Hotel in Bensalem, correct?"

"Yes," Petula said, getting comfortable in the back seat.

"Bensalem is a nice place."

"I know. I used to live there."

"Why did you move?"

"Wanted to try living someplace new."

Warm feelings came over Petula when she started spotting familiar sights, restaurants, strip malls and grocery stores on Street Road, a road she had driven down more times than she could count while she'd lived in Bensalem.

She couldn't have been happier when the Uber driver bumped his car into the parking lot at the Mango Hotel just off Street Road. She knew the area well. It gave her a comforting, safe feeling. She knew she was less than five miles from the Neshaminy Mall, even closer to the Franklin Mills Mall which was at the border of Bensalem and Philadelphia.

Using her Uber app, she tipped the driver twenty percent of the cost of the ride, then got out of the car. Warm rain came down on her shoulders like a light shower. When she felt rain dripping down the sides of her face, she opened the back passenger door again, returning to the car. "Can you drive me to the Franklin Mills Mall and wait? I need to get something. Then, can you drive me back to the hotel?"

"Sure."

As soon as she walked beneath the Franklin Mills Mall entrance, she looked up at the large forest green posts and the tall beige ceiling. Memories flooded her with peaceful assurance. By the time she reached the first food court, she was smiling. She wondered if the post office was still at the mall. That was the place from which she'd formerly mailed copies of the poetry book she'd written and self-published ten years ago.

Fashion designer outlets, discount shoe stores, video game stores, jewelers, department stores, sporting goods stores and a supermarket lined the sides of the walkway. Busy with shoppers, Petula dodged around other consumers as she made her way deeper inside the mall, bright lights overhead, popular music playing on the mall sound system.

When she walked out of the Franklin Mills Mall, it was still raining. Handles to two large shopping bags filled with blouses, t-shirts, jeans, a nightgown, socks, hygiene products and underwear straddled her hands.

The first words out of her mouth when she scooted across the back seat of the Uber car, shopping bags on the floor were, "Thank you." They were the same words she spoke to the Uber driver when he returned her to the Mango Hotel.

"My pleasure," the driver smiled at her.

Hurrying away from the car, she made her way toward the hotel. Checking in was easy, quick.

"I'm in Bensalem now," she texted Ariana after she entered her hotel room and placed the shopping bags on the floor. "This has been an eventful start to my vacation. Will tell you more about it later."

After she placed her cellphone on the nightstand, she relaxed into a warm bubble bath. Moments later, and feeling clean after the bath, her back didn't hurt when she pulled back the bed covers and climbed onto the clean, crisp hotel sheets. It was one of the amenities that she loved about sleeping at a hotel, the sheets were so clean and crisp, the way she remembered her paternal grandparents' sheets being at their house back in Ohio.

Tucked beneath the crisp bed sheets, she reached for the television remote control, and punching the power button, she turned on the flat screen television. She didn't check her cellphone for messages from Gloria. Right now, all she wanted to do was to relax, having spent most of the day in a state of stress and anxiety.

She was drifting toward sleep, her head sinking into the soft pillows, when Paul's face crossed her mind's eye. The remote again in her hand, she turned the volume down, threw back the bed covers and hurried across the floor to the nightstand. Picking up her cellphone, she opened a web browser and typed "Paul Gibbs, Army, Bucks County" into the search box. "Wonder what set Paul off when he saw me at the state forest. Maybe I remind him of someone who hurt him," she mused as her fingers sped across the cellphone panel.

Two rows of ribbons and medals lined the military uniform jacket that Paul wore in pictures that came up in the search. His hair was cut low, his face clean shaven, no sight of a beard. Instead of a smile, his mouth formed a straight line. In the pictures Paul looked serious to Petula, like he was always headed to war.

"Decorated calvary scout, marksman, computer enthusiasts, aviator, special forces weapons sergeant, and complex PTSDs" scrolled across the screen as Petula continued her search. She learned that Paul had entered the Army when he was only eighteen years old.

"Just a kid," Petula said to the empty hotel room, shaking her head. "But he's not a kid anymore," she frowned, reading the drunk driving charges that Paul had been convicted of over the last several years.

For the next ten minutes, she searched for news articles on Paul Gibbs. There were drunk driving and two burglary charges but no stories about Paul stalking a woman.

Tiring of thinking about Paul and weary with combating the painful blend of fear and fatigue, Petula returned her cellphone to the nightstand and climbed back into bed. Moments later, she leaned up on her forearms, her gaze shifting, searching for an answer in the dark room, and her voice uneven, she asked herself, "Why is Paul coming for me?"

## Chapter Eight

Birds were calling to each other and singing magnificent songs outside the hotel when Petula woke up the following morning, sunrays streaming through the part in the drapes, brightening the room. Pulling the comforter beneath her chin, she turned on her side and sunk her head into the goose down pillow. It surprised her how peacefully and how deeply she'd slept. Listening to the birds singing, she told herself that the day would be rewarding, as carefree and as peaceful as her sleep had been.

Closing her eyes and treasuring the pillow's softness, she even thought about visiting the Newtown shops. Before she knew it, she was thinking about the purple and green knee-length silk dress she'd bought from Sheer Design while she'd been in college, a favorite Newtown boutique of hers. She'd worn the dress to a concert she'd attended with Gloria and James and a guy she'd been dating for several months. Recalling the fun she'd had at the concert, she smiled. Then, feeling pressure in her lower stomach, she pulled back the comforter, sat up and hurried into the bathroom where she emptied her bladder and took a shower.

She felt so rejuvenated, free of worry and safe from trouble, that she dressed, grabbed her shoulder pocketbook and hotel key and exited the room, making her way to the elevators and the warmth of the morning sun. "Is there a café or restaurant where I can get a cup of tea?" she asked the valet who stood on the hotel's porch entranceway.

"Maas serves amazing African and Japanese teas," the valet told her. Pointing, he added, "It's right across the street, sandwiched between that candle shop and small bookstore."

"That's where I'm headed then. Thank you," Petula said. She'd rode her bicycle down this road more times than she could count while she'd lived in Bensalem.

Foot traffic was light, street traffic heavier as she made her way to the corner to cross the street. Iconic birch, glory maple and beautiful redbud trees stood at the back of the shops lining the street. As she neared Maas, scent from the trees wafted up her nose, filling her with a sense of wonder.

"Yesterday was troubling," she mused. "But today," she smiled, looking up at the trees, "is beautiful." Being in town versus at the forest brought her comfort. She took in the morning's quaintness, remembering why, while still in Atlanta planning her vacation, she'd chosen to visit Bensalem again, being satisfied with how open, clean and inviting the township was.

Nostalgia had such a grip on her that she kept looking about, taking in the trees, the few other pedestrians and the two pet dogs she passed as she crossed the street. Despite the light foot traffic and how unfamiliar scents, faces and buildings distracted her, feeding her curiosity, on her way inside Maas, she bumped into a thirtyish man and a grey-haired woman leaning on a cane. "Excuse me," she said, looking at the woman, fearful that she'd come close to knocking her off balance. After giving the woman a final look, ensuring that she was steady on her feet, Petula turned and entered the tea shop.

"Shikamoo," the Maas clerk, a brown shortie head wrap decorating her tall ponytail, greeted Petula upon her entrance into the tea shop.

"Good morning," Petula nodded, admiring the woman's rich ebony skin tone. "Do you have cherry tea?"

"This way," the clerk said, leaving the check-out counter and walking to the back of an aisle. "We have four different cherry teas," she told Petula, holding a decorative tea box up.

Petula leaned toward the raised box, and the clerk removed the lid, smiling as she watched Petula breath in the delightful scent.

Moments later, Petula was walking out of Maas, a bag filled with two boxes of cherry teas and a freshly steeped cup of Japanese cherry blossom tea in her hand. Returning to the Mango Hotel's porch area, she sat at a round, glass table that overlooked the outdoor swimming pool.

The tea was invitingly warm, not too hot, when she drank it. Made to offer a gentle blend, drinking the tea enticed Petula to settle into the gift of the new day. Residents and tourists not yet fully about, it was easy for her to appreciate being in the familiar small township, a place she'd once been honored to call 'home'.

Soon she was reaching inside her shoulder pocketbook, pulling out her cellphone and taking pictures of the hotel's outdoor grounds. Gardens of Oriental lilies, African violets, Hawaiian plumeria and English daisies demanded her attention, so much so that she took a dozen pictures of the gardens that were bursting with color.

Captured by the beauty, everyday sounds and movement around her, she turned away from the gardens and focused her attention on the sidewalks and street. Women chatted, flats and heels setting off their wardrobe, as they made their way to work. Men hurried toward offices, suit jacket and shirt and tie on, briefcase in hand. Sprinkled amid them, mothers and fathers pushed babies in strollers passed the hotel, further down the sidewalk.

Eager to capture the goings-on, Petula raised her cellphone and started taking pictures. Seconds later, she laughed, recalling how her maternal grandmother had always taken pictures of relatives when they visited her. "Stand over by the window," she recalled her grandmother saying. That or "Sit on the sofa. Sit up straight now and smile," she remembered her grandmother directing family.

She laughed at the memory before she gazed about her surroundings and said, "Now, I'm glad I came a few days before Gloria and James got home. It's good to be back in Bensalem," she whispered, sitting back in the chair and smiling. When she sat up, a red-haired man wearing a yellow shirt captured her attention.

She wondered if she'd seen him when she'd entered Maas, perhaps when she'd bumped into the elderly woman. His bold shirt color was familiar to her.

Feeling intrusive, she turned away from the man only to, seconds later, look across the street again. It startled her when she thought she saw the man looking right at her, as if she was the only person outside.

Above her, a bird squawked, and she turned her attention to the pictures on her cellphone. Curiosity strong, she peered up and across the street.

The man looked at her an instant longer then blended in with the other men and women making their way further into town. As she stood from the chair, the clerk at Maas stepped outside. She and Petula met glances and the clerk waved; Petula waved back then turned and entered the hotel carrying the cup of tea.

While she waited for the elevator, she told herself to stop thinking that everyone who stared at her meant her harm. "There's such a thing as a friendly stranger," she thought.

Back in her hotel room, she considered calling the front desk from the room phone and extending her stay at the hotel another two nights. But then habit intervened, and as she had done every morning for the past fifteen years, she picked up her cellphone, this time checking for messages.

There was a message from Gloria. "James and I are in Orlando. Our flight doesn't leave for another three days. But we will come home right now if you need us to. Please text me back asap and let me know that you're okay."

Petula saw that the text message had come while she'd been at Maas. Since she didn't want Gloria and James to worry more than she figured they already had, she called Gloria instead of texting her.

"Gloria," she said as soon as she heard her friend's voice cross the line.

"Petula," Gloria shouted. "Are you okay? I freaked out when I got your voice message last night."

"I'm okay. I'm at the Mango Hotel off Street Road in Bensalem, the one close to the Franklin Mills Mall."

"Good." Gloria paused. "Who was following you?"

"Some guy named Paul Gibbs."

"Where did you meet him?"

"I was at the state forest campgrounds—"

"—That's right. You did say that." After another pause, Gloria asked, "How did you get to the hotel?"

"I got an Uber".

"Smart," Gloria said. "Glad you got somewhere safe."

"Yes," Petula nodded. "So, are you having fun in Orlando?"

"Girl, yes."

"Well, I'm glad James and you didn't hop on a plane because of me. Don't come back early. I'll stay at the hotel for another two nights. We'll meet up like we had originally planned. I'll meet you at your place in another three days."

"No. No. No," Gloria said. "I'll come by and get you when we get back. You can stay with us until you're ready to head back to Atlanta. And what about your RV? Is it running?"

"No, it's not running. I'll call for repairs later today. I'll just have the repair shop tow the RV to a repair center, and I'll pick it up from there in a few days, just before I head back to Atlanta."

"James and I will go to the repair shop with you, especially after what happened with this guy you said was following you. That's creepy."

"Yeah. It is creepy," Petula said, looking at the television. Seconds later, she glanced toward the window.

"But I'm going to get my RV towed to a repair shop this morning. I want to know my rig is good to go sooner than later."

When she hung up from talking with Gloria, she raised her cellphone and prepared to dial the RV repair center Chris worked for, but she heard someone call out, "Hello" outside her hotel door.

"Who is it?" Petula asked, standing next to the bed, her gaze fixed on the door.

"Room service," a man's deep baritone voice answered.

"I didn't ask for room service," she told the man.

"Is another guest in the room?"

Petula stared at the door, becoming increasingly irritated at the man's unwillingness to accept her answer that she hadn't asked for room service. When she didn't hear the man moving away from her room, she raised her voice and ordered, "Get away from the door."

"What's your name?" the man asked, laughter in his voice.

"I didn't order room service," Petula shouted.

The man knocked on the door hard, pounding, rattling the door.

Petula raced to the phone and dialed the front desk, fixing her gaze on the door while she waited for the desk clerk to pick up.

"This is Room 634," she told the clerk.

"Yes. We can see which room is calling on the dashboard," the clerk told her. "How may I help you?"

"There's a man outside my room," she said, glancing at the bottom of the door. Although she wished that the man hadn't appeared, she was glad to still see his feet beneath the door. She didn't want the clerk to think that she had misspoken or was mentally imbalanced. "He said he's with room service, but I didn't call for room service."

"Let me check your outgoing calls. I'm going to put you on a brief hold."

While she waited for the clerk to return to the line, Petula closed her eyes and hung her head. She retraced her steps; the only person she'd told that she was staying at the Mango Hotel was Gloria and they'd just spoken. "No one else knows I'm here," she mused. Then, she figured that the man outside her door was mistaken; he simply had the wrong room. What she couldn't figure was why he was still standing outside her room. Revisiting yesterday's danger, she started hunting for a clue as to why odd unwanted encounters with strange men were happening to her.

When she'd left for vacation, Veronica had been accusing her of trying to sabotage her records and steal her clients. But Petula had been certain that she'd put that behind her before she'd hopped inside her RV and headed up the road, driving further away from work in Atlanta. "Oh, forget it," she thought. "I can't go off the deep end connecting one unfortunate event to another." Opening her eyes and raising her head, she thought, "Let me just focus on why this guy showed up at my hotel room. For all I know, it's not a big thing but that guy did start pounding on my door."

The clerk's voice broke up her thoughts. "You're right," the clerk said after she took the phone off 'hold'. "You didn't call for room service, at least not from your room phone you didn't. I checked the restaurant too. Would you like me to send security to your room?"

"Please."

"Security is on the way," the desk clerk said a moment later. "You'll see a man and a woman dressed in our hotel's gray and red uniforms. They are from security."

"Thank you."

"The man's name is Floyd. The woman's name is Leontyne."

"Thank you. I appreciate you sharing that."

Petula hung up the telephone and waited, her eye against the peep hole. Moments later, she saw the man hurry away from her door and run down the hallway. Her breath caught in her throat as she watched his yellow shirt puffing outward as air pushed down the shirt while he ran.

She didn't release a deep breath until she looked through the peep hole and saw the two security guards on the other side. Before she had time to consider what had caused the guy to flee, the telephone rang. Hurrying to the writing table that the telephone was placed on, she snatched the receiver out of the cradle. "Hello?"

"It's the front desk."

"Yes?"

"Have the two security personnel arrived?"

"Yes. They're in the hallway now. I'll go let them in."

There was a lull in the conversation. Then, the desk clerk said, "Okay. Call back if you need anything else."

Petula returned to the door, squinting through the peep hole for only seconds when she unlocked the door.

"Yes?" Petula said, peering through a crack in the open door.

"We're from security," Leontyne said. "You called the front desk for security, correct?"

"Yes." Slowly opening the door more, giving Leontyne and Floyd room to enter, Petula peered down the hallway. It was empty.

Following Petula's gaze, Leontyne asked, "Is it okay if we come in and make sure you're okay?"

Petula nodded, "Sure." Peering into the hallway again, she asked, "Where did the guy go?"

Floyd turned back toward the door, "The hallway was empty when we reached your room."

Glancing at Floyd then at Petula, Leontyne said, "The guy who'd knocked on your door probably took off when he saw us. We'll search the floor before we leave the area."

"Let me go check around the ice machine and the balcony area," Floyd said.

As Floyd walked to the door, Leontyne shrugged. "This is a nice hotel but, every now and then someone who's up to no good comes through. It's very rare," she assured Petula.

Petula walked into the hallway, tempted to shadow Floyd so she could see for herself that the guy was long gone. But she didn't follow Floyd, leaning against the doorway, her gaze fixed on the exit that led to the ice machine.

Her chest felt tight until she saw Floyd round the corner, a slight smile on his face. "Whoever was at your door appears to be gone. Since Leontyne and I didn't see him, figure he hurried around the corner to the ice machine and then around the corner halfway down the back hall to the elevator."

Petula crossed her arms, then quickly uncrossed them. "I guess," she sighed, following Floyd inside her hotel room.

"How long have you been at the hotel?" Floyd began.

"Last night was my first night."

"And you didn't order room service last night or this morning?"

"No," Petula answered him.

"Could just be an innocent mistake," Floyd suggested. "Maybe he meant to go to another room."

"Then, why would he take off? And," she added, looking at the floor, "he was wearing a yellow shirt, similar to the shirt the guy across the street from the hotel was wearing when I'd gone outside to get a cup of tea this morning."

"Did you tell the guy who came to your room that he had the wrong room?" Floyd asked, peering into the bathroom.

"I did, but he wouldn't leave. He even started pounding on my door which is when I called the front desk."

"We'll make rounds here several times a day and during the night," Floyd told her. "Your and every guest's safety is our priority."

"Thank you," Petula stammered, swallowing hard, eager to feel like she really was safe.

While Floyd asked Petula a series of questions, Leontyne walked to the window and looked out, as if checking for something on the street.

Petula watched Leontyne at the window while she nodded into the answers she gave Floyd. Back and forth she diverted her attention, focusing mainly on what Floyd was asking. Finally, she told him, "Like I told you before, I've never had contact with the guy who showed up saying he was from room service. Weird things have been happening to me since I showed up in this area yesterday." Shaking her head, she added, "It's been one thing after another."

Leontyne looked over her shoulder at Petula. "Come here."

"Did you see which way the guy went when he left?" Floyd asked Petula. "Did he go in another room on this floor?"

"He ran down the hall," Petula said. "I didn't open the door. I could only see so far down the hall. He was carrying a bag."

"Come here," Leontyne looked over her shoulder and told Petula again.

Petula ran her hand back and forth across her forehead, working to calm her nerves. "Maybe I should have run after him—"

"—No," Floyd told her. "You did the right thing by staying in your room and calling us. I just didn't know if you had opened the door to talk with the guy after he knocked."

"Come here," Leontyne tried again, almost demanding that Petula join her at the window.

"What is it?" Petula asked, walking across the floor and standing next to Leontyne.

"The guy in the pizza delivery vehicle is gone now," she told Petula as soon as she stepped alongside her, craning her neck and looking out the window onto the street. "I was going to see if the delivery driver is the guy who came to your room. I know you said the guy said he was from room service, but I'm checking all bases."

Seconds later, Petula stood by the window watching Floyd and Leontyne leave her room and return to the hallway. Everything felt surreal to her, as if the last two days were a bad dream.

"I'm going to check the floor one last time," Floyd told Petula.

"Thank you," Petula smiled. "Last thing I want is for that guy to have hid somewhere and then come back out after he thinks you're gone."

Petula walked to the door's edge and watched the goings-on in the hallway, Leontyne and Floyd knocking on doors and checking the ice machine area again. Then, turning away from the door, she reentered her room, staring at the ceiling.

She stood looking at the ceiling for several seconds, as if seeking answers, when she felt a presence at the doorway, a quiet specter, someone preparing to enter her room with stealth. "Leontyne! Floyd!" she screamed as soon as she turned and saw the man standing behind her.

## Chapter Nine

Heart pounding, she ran to the door, desperate to catch the man who'd been standing inside her hotel room then taken off after she screamed. She wanted to confront him, end the fear—but dread pulled her back. As she hurried to the other side of the door, standing in the hallway, the man's back grew distant, and she was torn between relief and rising terror.

Within seconds, she heard Floyd's and Leontyne's feet thundering down the hall, toward her room.

Petula braced her hand against the door's edge as she watched the guy who'd come to her door earlier search for an exit. To Petula, it was as if he was a ghost, the way he disappeared and reappeared.

"Stop," she heard Floyd shout at the guy. "Come here."

Turning and facing Petula, Leontyne asked, "Is this the guy who said you'd ordered room service?"

"Yes," Petula said, her forehead burrowing into a deep frown.

"Where did you get off to earlier?" Floyd asked the guy. "And what's your name?"

"I don't want any trouble," the guy said.

"What's your name?" Floyd repeated.

The man looked at Floyd; his response was quick. "Dale Stewart."

Petula's hands clenched the door jamb. "Why did you come to my room?"

Dale looked at her but didn't speak.

"Why did you come to my room?" she shouted.

Dale lowered his head. When he looked up again, he told her, "I had the wrong room." He smiled. "I apologize."

"No," Petula said, shaking her head. "No. No," she continued, walking toward Dale. "It's not that simple. You came here for a reason. You lied and said you were from room service when you're not. You didn't just come here. This isn't an accident. I saw you outside after I left Maas," she told him, now in his face. "You meant to come here. That bag is just a decoy just like you lying about being from room service is a lie. I can see from here that bag is empty. Like I asked you before, why did you come to my room?"

He stepped forward, close enough to brush noses with her if he leaned forward, "Like I told you," he said, glaring at her. "It was an accident. I already apologized for disturbing you. I had the wrong room." Glancing at Floyd and Leontyne, he said, "They get it and they're with hotel security." Stepping back, he peered down at her and frowned. "I don't know why you can't get it."

"I don't get it because I'm the target, damn it."

"Okay. You're going to be disrespectful," Dale told her. "You probably don't even respect yourself. For some reason, you can't accept that I simply came to the wrong room. Seeing you now," he shrugged. "I regret coming to your room. You're not a woman worth respect."

Petula's next words came out even, hard. "Why-did-you-come-to-my-room?"

Leontyne watched Dale closely. Floyd glanced at him with curiosity.

"Had the wrong room."

"No, you didn't. You come here with an empty bag saying you're from room service, like I called for you, and you want me to believe it's all an accident?"

Dale sighed, then he turned away from Petula and laughed. Before he returned his attention to her, he looked at Leontyne and Floyd, as if awaiting their approval. "It was all a joke."

"That's your next best try?" Petula scowled.

Dale turned to Floyd. "May I go now?"

Petula stepped forward. "No. I'm calling the police."

Leontyne and Floyd gave each other a wary glance. "We'll take him downstairs and make a report," Leontyne told her.

"I'm calling the police," Petula said. She was firm. Instead of calling the police from the hotel phone, she speed-dialed the police using her cellphone. As soon as the police desk clerk came on the line, she said, "This is the woman who came into the police station with Officer Duggan yesterday, the woman whose RV had broken down."

"Yes."

"Can you send an officer to the Mango Hotel just off Street Road? There's a safety situation here." She looked at Leontyne and Floyd, angry that they hadn't been rough with Dale, demanded that he exit the hotel immediately. "Hotel security may be unable to resolve the situation."

"Are you in danger? Is this a criminal matter?"

"I don't know. A guy named Dale Stewart came to my hotel room, knocked on the door and said he was from room service." Looking at Dale, she continued, "He doesn't even work at the hotel."

"Doesn't sound like something the police can get involved with. Work with hotel security. Is hotel security with you now?"

"Yes."

"Put them on please."

Instead of handing her cellphone to Leontyne or Floyd, she pressed the speaker button. "The police officer wants to talk with you," she told them.

"Hello, this is Leontyne Marks. I'm one of the two security guards with the guest."

"And I'm Floyd Jackson, the other security guard."

"Do you have this issue under control?"

"We're going to take the guy downstairs and file a report. We'll also file a copy of the report with the police department."

"Okay."

Petula couldn't believe how smoothly the conversation was going. "Don't you want to know why this guy named Dale lied about being with room service? He didn't just come to my door. He was even trying to make it sound like an accident." She looked at Dale while she spoke to the police officer. "Who shows up at someone's hotel room lying about being from room service and carrying an empty bag? He just wanted me to open the door."

"Hotel security, file the report," the police officer said. "Mr. Dale, stay away from the guest. If you're seen around the guest and she files a report, you'll be picked up. Do you understand?"

"Yes."

"Leontyne and Floyd, you said it was?" the police officer asked.

"Yes," Floyd told him.

"Make sure you file the report and be thorough."

"We will," Floyd assured.

The line went dead.

For an instant, Petula felt she had no choice except to watch Dale, Leontyne and Floyd walk away from her to the front desk. Then, she grabbed her shoulder pocketbook, shoved her cellphone inside the pocketbook's wide pouch, grabbed her hotel room key and headed for the elevator.

What she saw when she reached a faraway corner of the lobby brought her relief. She watched Leontyne and Floyd enter a small office with Dale. Then, moments later, she watched Dale exit the hotel, Leontyne and Floyd giving him a stern warning not to return to the premises.

As soon as Petula reached her hotel room again, she laid her key on the table, grabbed her belongings and shoved them in the shopping bags. She was at the door's edge when she remembered her hotel key.

Spotting the key on the table, she went to the bed, then sat and closed her eyes. Before she knew it, she was dialing Ariana's cellphone. She clenched her jaw while she listened to her sister's phone ring.

Then, she leaned back on the bed and sighed before she heard Ariana say, "Jambo?"

"Hey, Sis. It's me, Petula."

"You sound tired."

"I feel tired, at least right now I do." Glancing at the door, she continued, "Remember that guy I told you about who I thought was standing outside my apartment when I lived in Bensalem years ago?"

"Don't tell me he's come back on the scene?"

"Oh, no. He did that that one time and I never saw or heard from him again."

"Good." After a pause, Ariana asked, "So, what's up?"

"I'm sure this is going to turn into a really nice vacation," Petula tried.

"Petula?"

"I'm okay. I'm safe." Seconds later, she sighed and relinquished her quest to protect Ariana from worry, sacrificing the urge to share her plight more fully to keep her sister from stress. "I'm lying. Best as I can tell, I'm okay. A strange guy showed up at my hotel room."

"What—" Ariana hollered.

"—Don't you go worrying," Petula advised. "That's why I lied to you before. I don't want you to worry and make yourself sick, driving your blood pressure up into the 170s like it was a year ago when you were working crazy hours, pushing yourself way too hard. You know I know how to take care of myself. I'll be okay," she told Ariana while she glanced from the window to the door, her hands trembling.

"Forget me and my blood pressure. Is someone being a jerk with you?" Before Petula could answer, she asked, "Did your job tell you to cut your vacation short and come back to the office?"

"No," Petula said. "Some guy was being weird when I was at the state forest campgrounds. So, I left there. Like I texted you, I'm in Bensalem."

"I know you said Gloria and her husband are coming home in a few days. Until they get there, good thing you know Bensalem. You lived there for years, so fortunately it's not a strange place."

"True, but strange things have been happening and I can't get it out of my head that the guy at the campgrounds had a Custom Accounting Designs keychain. Those are branded items that are only ordered through our firm's marketing department. You can't get those keychains at a department store."

"Who at Custom Accounting Designs do you think would know that guy you saw at the campgrounds?"

Petula shrugged. "I don't know. I work in the Atlanta office, miles from here."

"It is weird about the guy having the keychain. Did he show it off like he wanted you to know he had it?"

After a pause, Petula said. "In a way, I think he did."

"Petula, I'm glad you left the campgrounds. You don't want some dude who's being creepy zoning in on you."

Looking at the door then out the window, she nodded. "Yes. It's just a lot of weird stuff happening. Feel like I must figure out what's really going on. I've got to get to the bottom of this. I don't want to start linking every single event, but I can't get the fact that the guy at the campground has some connection to work."

"Custom Accounting Designs is a national company, Petula. Maybe the guy is a customer, and his representative gave him the keychain."

"Maybe," Petula sighed.

"Don't read too much into this."

"I'm trying not to."

"Is there something you haven't told me?" Ariana asked.

"Ariana, I don't want to worry you. I'm probably over thinking things. I filed a police report against the guy at the campgrounds, so I shouldn't see him again."

"The guy was stalking you like that?"

Chewing her fingernail, she said, "He was paying me way too much attention."

"Where did you say you are now?"

"I'm in my hotel room."

"Where are you staying?"

"At the Mango Hotel. It's in a good spot right off Street Road. It's close to the Franklin Mills Mall. I took you there when you visited me when I was living in Bensalem."

"I remember," Ariana nodded. "I always liked visiting you in Bensalem." She paused; when she spoke again, there was heaviness in her voice. "Don't lie to me to try to protect me. Do you really feel safe?"

Before answering, Petula looked toward the door and sighed. "I feel better."

"That's good." There was a pause. "I'll come down there today if you're not safe."

"I'm safe," Petula said, glancing at the room door.

"Have you been to Bensalem, Philadelphia or visited any shops?"

"I may get to Newtown today," she sighed, not wanting to trouble Ariana with details about the Dale Stewart guy, angry with herself for being in the situation she found herself in. She couldn't count the times Ariana had advised her not to vacation alone, but of the two of them, Petula knew that Ariana was the more cautious one. Living alone and honoring her independence found Petula taking on more risks, daring to live the life she truly wanted to live even if it put her alone in iffy situations. But yesterday at the campgrounds then at Chris' followed by the guy who'd come to her hotel room left her unnerved.

"Petula, are you really okay?" Ariana asked.

"I'll be okay," Petula said, speaking slowly, evenly. "Just wanted to call and hear your voice. Haven't been up here to this area in a minute. So much of it is familiar. So much seems brand new."

"Like Mama and Dad taught us, that's how life is in this world. Change. Change. Change."

Petula nodded. "Yes."

"Just stay sharp and call me if you need anything."

"Are you at work?"

"Yes. I'm on break. Always have time to talk with my sister, though."

"Still keeping long hours?" Petula asked, not yet ready to end the call.

"I'm at work by seven in the morning and home by five or six o'clock, but I log on after I get dinner and spend time with Leon and the girls, but only for about another one to two hours. It's just so busy at work right now."

"I feel you," Petula said, comforted by Ariana's voice. "Well, let me let you go, so you can chill and enjoy the rest of your break."

"Cool. Like I said earlier, call me if you need anything."

"I will. And, hey, tell Leon and the girls I said 'hi'. Same goes for you too. Call me if you need anything. Love you, Ariana."

She was standing, when Ariana said, "Love you too."

Comforted by the thought that she would be okay, simply because she'd heard a familiar voice, had been boosted by the support of someone she knew genuinely cared about her, Petula laid her cellphone on the table, next to her room key, then sat on the bed's edge. It surprised her how her encounter with Dale had shifted her mood, howbeit strengthened her resolve to get to the bottom of why she was being followed.

She sat on the bed, gazing across the empty room, looking toward the window, wondering what was going to happen next. She wondered if she should stay in Bensalem until she knew why Paul and Dale were after her. If she did, she knew she'd have to keep a low profile, move through the township like a phantom.

A second later, she stood and reached for the hotel door key. It fell to the floor. Bending to pick up the key, she bumped her head on the table, the thrust of which knocked her cellphone off the table's edge.

"What's this?" she wondered out loud as she pulled a tiny black metal object away from the back of her cellphone.

When she looked at the gadget beneath the room light, she realized that it was a tracking device. "What in the world," she stammered. She turned the tracker in her hand. "Who put this behind my cellphone cover and how long has it been here?"

She wondered if the tracker was placed on her cellphone after she came to the hotel. She wondered if someone had gotten her cellphone when she was distracted at Maas or the mall, placed the tracker on her phone and returned it to her pant pocket or shoulder pocketbook pouch. The more she thought about it, the less she believed that could have occurred. "It would take a serious pickpocket, someone who had made a career out of committing heists, to pull that off," she mused. She couldn't help but wonder how long the tracker would have remained on her cellphone if she hadn't bumped the table, knocking her cellphone to the floor, forcing the back cover away from the phone.

Using the tip of a writing pen and giving the back of her cellphone several hard bangs against the table's edge, she broke the tracking device away from her phone. Then, she put the device in her shoulder pocketbook, grabbed the key and her cellphone and headed for the door, her mind heavy, troubled.

Chapter Ten

Fifteen minutes later, the Mango Hotel doors were closing when Petula sprinted into the parking lot, the afternoon sun casting golden light beams across the asphalt. "Gloria! James!" she shouted, laughter drifting on the noonday breeze. Her heart surged. The days spent without her friends in Bensalem had begun to feel like a weight bearing down upon her, growing heavier with each passing day. No longer facing challenges alone, their return lit her up with relief, hope and tranquility. Her sneakers pounded the pavement as she ran, smiling so wide her face hurt, her arms reaching out for her friends.

"We got here as soon as we could," Gloria said, wrapping her arms around Petula, squeezing her tight. "As soon as we got home, we dropped our suitcases on the living room floor and headed back out the door," she continued, releasing Petula but still smiling at her. "We would have come sooner if you had asked us to."

"I didn't want to break up your vacation." Petula inhaled deeply, her chest going out like a balloon filling up with air. She looked at Gloria. "I feel so much better now that you both are here."

Seconds later, she released a slow breath. "My RV was towed a couple of mornings ago. It's in the repair shop." Determined not to let three strange encounters ruin her vacation, she stood straight, head back and added, "Hopefully, we can get to Philly, Newtown, the Neshaminy State Park and maybe even catch the train to Manhattan and watch a play over the next few days."

"Sounds great. For now, let's hop in our Benz and grab a bite for lunch," Gloria offered. "Does that sound good?" she asked, glancing across her shoulder at Petula.

"Sounds good." Moments later, the Mercedes-Benz was speeding further into town. Looking through the front windshield where she sat next to Gloria who busied herself driving while James sat in the back seat, Petula continued, "Not a lot of people were at the forest when I arrived, but I didn't want to leave my RV there until you got back, not that my rig looks like a prize anymore."

"You were smart to get it to a shop," Gloria said, craning her neck and looking through the top of the window, watching darkening clouds move like an eclipse across the fading sun. "And it's a good thing we got here when we did. The sky is getting suddenly dark." She shrugged. "It was so beautiful less than ten minutes ago. Now it looks like it's about to storm."

Soon wind gusts were pushing against the car, betraying the remaining bits of sunrays, creating a whistling noise as Petula, Gloria and James caught each other up on their latest happenings.

"It's not pouring rain yet but looks like it's about to start really coming down any second," Petula said. "Are James and you cool with lunching at Amble Taste? It's less than three blocks from here."

James leaned across the back seat, peering through the front seat dividers. "Yes. Let's go to Amble Taste. We don't want to get caught in a thunderstorm."

Nodding, Gloria said, "Amble's has the best seafood and pasta." She bumped Petula's elbow. "Remember when we'd order those big shrimp bowls from Amble's while we were in college?"

"Yeah," Petula responded, her voice low and faint, her thoughts distant. Try as she might, she couldn't stop thinking about her rig and how much it was going to cost to repair it so she could get back on the road. "Tho-those were fun times," she smiled, her lips barely curling up at the edges.

Gloria frowned when she looked at Petula. "Your mind is back at that forest." After a pause, she asked, "How many times did that guy ram his van into the back of your RV?"

"How many times?" Petula echoed. She looked at her friend. "Enough times."

Gloria tapped the top of Petula's hand. "The repair shop will get your RV in great shape in no time." Shaking her head, she added, "Your RV is one sweet ride."

"Looks like a small apartment," James said, "I remember when we visited you in Atlanta a few months ago. Your RV has a nice living room. I was digging on that wide screen television."

After they pulled into Amble Taste's parking lot, James asked Gloria, "Would you like one of those rigs?"

"Would be great to travel in, and the way we go from coast to coast, traveling from Bensalem all the way down to Florida and all the way to New York, could be a great choice, not to mention a good way to save on hotel expenses."

"That's one of the reasons I bought the RV. It's been good living, all until now," Petula sighed. "You don't want to see the bedroom." She gazed through the windshield at the rain, thoughts about the forest incident flooding her mind. Even as her mind's eye retrieved vivid memories of the damage done to her rig, she wondered if she could forget what had happened to her since she'd arrived in Pennsylvania and New Jersey; she wondered if she could enjoy a relaxing lunch with her friends and later visit Center City Philadelphia, behaving as if nothing had happened. She wondered if she could try to enjoy several more days of vacation then head back to Atlanta, walking into work as if she'd never seen Paul or had a run in with Dale at the hotel. Seconds later, she told herself that it was magical thinking to believe she could behave as if nothing had happened and that, if she was going to get to the bottom of why Paul and Dale were after her, she had best face reality.

"So much stuff fell to the floor from the van hits," Petula said, turning away from looking out the window and facing Gloria, who had just pulled inside Amble Taste's parking lot and turned the car engine off. "But figurines, cologne bottles and other personal items being tossed on the floor isn't enough to prove that Paul had caused the damage, and my mind wasn't focused on going back to the forest that night, looking for more evidence or trying to prove anything. I just wanted to find a safe place to spend the night. And besides, nobody else was in the area of the state forest I was in when he was ramming my RV, not a single witness in sight. It would have just been my word against his. If Ashleigh and her husband, Byron, the couple I met at the campgrounds were still here, they'd confirm that I had been leery of Paul." She pursed her lips. "But that still wouldn't prove anything. It wouldn't be probable cause. That's the thing," she sighed, looking at Gloria then James. "I don't have a way to prove half the stuff that's happened since I got up here."

Gloria leaned across the seat and wrapped her arm around Petula's shoulder. "You're going to get through this."

"Yes," James assured. "You're with friends now."

"That's part of what kept me going," Petula said, her head tucked beneath her jacket hood, as they made their way inside Amble Taste. "I knew I'd soon have good friends with me."

Despite retirees and college students filling much of Amble Taste, Petula, Gloria and James found an empty table next to a window midway into the restaurant. The afternoon waitress, a tall narrow woman with dreadlocks, came to take their orders as soon as they sat.

"Greek salad," Gloria told the waitress, not needing to review the menu.

"That's your favorite dish here," James laughed, looking across the table at Gloria and Petula.

"It is," Gloria nodded. "And what are you having, your go-to rice and garlic shrimp with tomatoes and cheese dish?"

James was still laughing when he looked up at the waitress and said, "I'll have what my wife said, the rice and garlic shrimp with tomatoes and cheese dish."

Leaning toward the window, Petula said, "You two still dine here as much as you did when we were in college?" Before they answered she added, "If you do, I can see why. The prices are as low as they were when we came here while we were broke in college."

"We were broke when we were in college," Gloria chimed. "Fortunately, things have changed. Now if we come here, it's solely for the food." Turning to the side, she asked Petula, "What are you having?"

"I'll take the cherry glazed salmon with a tossed salad," she told the waitress.

"Got it," the waitress said as she poured fresh ice water into the empty glasses on the table. Then, grabbing their menus, she stepped away from them.

While their food was being prepared, Petula, Gloria and James engaged in light conversation, mostly reliving the fun they'd had in college. By the time the waitress returned with their food, they were laughing about the afternoon they'd spent sledding downhill on a foot of snow while sitting on large plastic tops during their senior year of college.

Their meals -- bright with tomatoes, green peppers and tender beneath lingering stove heat -- on the table and the waitress on the other side of the restaurant, James jabbed his fork into his rice and garlic shrimp. "Besides the unfortunate encounter with the guy at the state forest," he began, his mouth full of food, "how have things been with you?"

Petula tossed her head from side to side while she chewed a bite of salmon, savoring the glazed cherry flavor, "Like I said earlier, now that my rig is in the repair shop, I feel better. Looking forward to hanging out with you two for the next few days."

Gloria bit into her Greek salad, then reached for her glass of water. "How are things at work? Are you still handling the larger accounts, including local government and mid-sized business accounts?" Before Petula answered, she added, "You've thrived since you relocated to the Atlanta office. Looks like the relocation was a good career move."

"Yes. I'm still handling those accounts. I prefer the government contracts most as they are less complex and easier to keep up with, not to mention how easy they are to audit." She bit into a forkful of salmon. "How are things at the hedge fund where you work, James?"

As if it was merely a habit, James glanced at Gloria. "It's a busy time at the hedge fund. Like I imagine you are at Custom Accounting Designs, we've been opening and managing lots of accounts, but it never seems like enough."

"What do you mean?" Petula asked.

"Higher ups push us to broker more large, complex deals. It feels like the pressure to broker deals with high-net-worth clients and pension funds is growing."

Shrugging, Petula offered, "Wonder if expenses at the hedge fund are increasing." She laughed. "Hedge fund portfolio managers aren't inexpensive, you know. A lot of times that's what drives senior leaders to push for large, complex contracts." She took a drink of water. "Just don't get caught up in the cycle of rushing to land accounts."

Gloria glanced at James. She twisted her mouth and asked Petula, "Why?"

"Because a bad account could cost a firm a lot more money than the overall deal would bring in over the life of the contract." She chewed on a forkful of salad. "It's not worth it." Turning toward Gloria, she asked, "Are things calmer at the venture capital firm where you work, good but calmer?"

"They are," Gloria nodded. "But I'd rather that things were busy. Wished that I was closing more deals." She laughed into, "More deals on my end equals bigger commissions and a bigger year-end bonus."

"That's true," Petula nodded. "Not that James and you need more loot. You both travel wherever you want and you wear the finest clothes. Both of you have set yourselves up nicely over the years." Glancing out the window, watching rain bounce against the glass then go long down the pane, she said, "You're a loving couple who have each other and who've managed to achieve your goals."

"We do live comfortably," Gloria admitted, picking up a piece of diced cucumber and running it through the rest of her salad, as if she was playing with her food. "But living comfortably comes with a price."

"I keep telling you both to pull back on spending," Petula joked. "High living will keep you two working 60 to 80 hours a week."

After he glanced at his wife, James looked toward the table and rolled his eyes. "We're living in a hustle culture, if you haven't noticed, Petula."

"Oh. I've noticed," Petula told him, bumping Gloria's elbow. "Gloria and I both are up on the hustle culture. Still, that doesn't mean that we all can't pull back," she added. "Which is why I'm on this vacation. Weeks ago, I realized that I had to relax. Can't keep going nonstop and avoid burnout."

"Speaking of burnout, Petula, what licenses are you required to have to handle government accounts? I've got to get the Series 7 if I want another promotion," Gloria revealed. "And you know how much study time is required to pass those licensing exams."

"I have a professional liability insurance license and a cyber liability insurance license," Petula told her. "I got those when I was still at the Bensalem office. Thinking about getting my Series 7. Licenses are required to work on most Custom Accounting Design accounts. We see a lot. I've seen enough data on some accounts that it's reached the point where I feel like I could write some clients' biographies."

James bit into his shrimp and rice. "Do you work with third party accounts?"

"No," Petula answered, shaking her head. "The accounts I work on at Custom Accounting Designs are straightforward. Only the most senior people at the firm are permitted to work on third party accounts and those employees work in New York City at the firm's headquarters. There's a tremendous amount of transparency, due diligence and oversight required on third party accounts." Shaking her head, she said, "I wouldn't want to touch third party accounts for anything, too risky."

Gloria ate the last bites of her salad. "Why?"

Looking at Gloria, Petula said, "It's easier to hide dirty money within third party accounts." After she drank some water, she looked from James to Gloria, then said, "It's probably the same way where you work."

"Yes," James nodded. "We run account checks all the time."

"Never know when compliance or an internal audit team is going to show up and start digging through records," Gloria shared. "That's why you have to be careful."

Their plates empty, the waitress approached their table. "May I remove the dishes?"

"Sure," Petula said, standing. "We're getting ready to head back outside. Thank you for the good service. It always feels somewhat like home here."

"Yes, thank you," Gloria smiled at the waitress. "We love dining here."

"We're happy to hear that," the waitress said, stepping away from their table with a trayful of empty plates and glasses.

Gloria and James followed the waitress, paying the bill and leaving a tip at the cash register on their way out the door. Behind them, Petula nodded at the cashier as she left a folded ten-dollar bill on the counter, ballooning the tip.

Moments later, Petula sat in the back seat of Gloria's and James' emerald, green Mercedes-Benz, her stomach full. "Thank you so much for coming to get me and for treating me to lunch. That salmon hit the spot."

"Glad you enjoyed lunch, and, about coming to get you, James and I wouldn't have it any other way," Gloria told her from where she sat up front in the car's passenger seat next to her husband. "We had to ensure you're okay and we still have a lot of vacation ahead of us," she smiled. They were pulling out of Amble Taste's parking lot, when she asked, "How are things with you and that woman at work?"

Closing her eyes, Petula sat back, as if she was waiting for a critical idea to surface, as if time had slowed, giving her a chance to think. In her mind's eye, she saw Veronica, recalled her flaunting a soft red and black

Yoruba women's skirt suit on her first day at the Atlanta office. Veronica had been walking toward her, a gentle smile stretching her face.

"Welcome," Veronica had said, her hand extended toward Petula, on Petula's first day at the Atlanta office. "We've been expecting you. Everyone at the Bensalem office brags about how good you are which is why we're glad you transferred to Atlanta."

Petula smiled at the compliment. "Custom Accounting Designs' Bensalem team is cool. I appreciate them putting in a good word for me, and I plan to live up to the hype."

"I hope you do," Veronica smiled. "But Atlanta isn't Bensalem. It's rougher down here."

The loud burst of laughter Petula erupted with gave her surprise. Regret and embarrassment blended, sending her stepping back as if seeking protection from potential disapproval from Veronica, a woman she scarcely knew.

"Stick with me," Veronica had smiled, twirling her pearl necklace around her index finger. "I'll show you around the city and teach you the ropes at the Atlanta office, including who our primary clients are. You'll be up to speed making big commissions and bonuses in no time."

"Thank you," Petula smiled again, feeling as if she was looking at a friend.

Months later, the relocation novelty faint, merely a wisp in her life, the tables turned. Petula had been dining for lunch at an upscale seafood restaurant in Buckhead with Bale Abara, plan administrator for the Service Leaders Retirement Fund. The lighting was soft, gentle. Soothing jazz played overhead, giving the restaurant an elegant ambience. Her laptop resting on the table corner, Petula discussed using cash value life insurance to finance the partnership agreement Bale had with his law firm's co-founder. She answered Bale's questions, digging into permanence, payout arrangements and savings growth – created a business briefing cadence that found her and Bale stretching lunch across an entire hour.

Less than twenty minutes passed after Petula returned to Custom Accounting Designs' corporate Atlanta complex following the lunch when Veronica stormed inside her office. "Why Bale Abara? Why are you going after him?"

Even now, from where she sat in the back of James' and Gloria's Benz, Petula could see herself turning toward the door. She had taken a step back when Veronica closed then locked the door.

"Bale is a plan administrator. There are several partners working on the fund—"

Veronica walked to within inches of Petula, towering over her. "--You are not going to have another conversation with Bale."

"Is that a threat—"

Pointing her finger at Petula, she tightened her face. "--No wonder the Bensalem office agreed to transfer you down here. You earn what you get off the sweat of other people's hard work and you don't know how the game's played."

Petula didn't blink. "I asked for a transfer because I wanted to move to Atlanta, and I did and still do my job as well as anybody. And," she added, standing up straighter, "I don't play games." Shaking her head slowly, she added, "I'm not going to be like you. We both may have started out small, struggling to find our way, working hard to land good clients, but I'm not taking shortcuts like you did. You could have won the right way, doing the right things." She shook her head. "Admittedly, when I first got here and even while I was in Bensalem and I heard how well you were doing, I wanted to mirror you, but not anymore." She swallowed hard, choking back regret's distaste. "We will never be the same."

Veronica's laugh sounded like a dry snort. She gave Petula a hard glare, then she turned and walked out of Petula's office.

**\*\*\*\*\*\*\*\*\*\***

Her thoughts no longer back at the Atlanta complex, Petula lowered her head and sighed. "Oh, Gloria, the woman you asked me about is Veronica Boyd." She raised her head. "My manager, a guy named Arthur Morgan, finally got the courage to talk with her about her on-the-job bullying." She shook her head. "I couldn't afford to fight Veronica, even though I think that's what she was pushing me to do. If I had done that, probably would have lost my job."

"For sure," James nodded. "That or if you really fought her and struck her, you might have gotten hit with a felony charge."

"Everybody else on the job is cool. I've never had a problem with anyone else at work."

"Where did you say Veronica is from?" Gloria wanted to know.

"You know, come to think of it," Petula said, "I think she's from around here."

Gloria paused, deep in thought, her voice trailing, going soft as she said, "You were living in Bensalem when you started working at the accounting firm." She chuckled. "The past never leaves us."

Petula followed Gloria's hazy stare. It landed on the passenger window's top corner. "You and James were the ones who told me to apply for work at Custom Accounting Designs' Atlanta office." She smiled, hoping to regain Gloria's full attention, pulling her away from wherever her mind had gone. "Thanks for suggesting that I put in for a transfer to work at their Atlanta office when I got to Atlanta years ago. It is a good firm. They pay me more than I've ever made working anywhere else. I couldn't afford to live in my Sandy Springs townhouse if I didn't work at Custom Accounting Designs, and I love my townhouse."

"Your townhouse is beautiful," Gloria smiled. "And spacious. You've got one glorious outdoor view from your living room."

"Yes," Petula beamed. "Sometimes I sit on the porch looking across that lush, wooded area. In the winter, I've seen deer pass through there." She glanced out the side window. "Cost a pretty penny to stay there. Fortunately, what I make at Custom Accounting Designs makes it easy to pay my rent, build my savings and do things I enjoy."

"Good," Gloria nodded. "Life's about more than work. You've got to enjoy life. You've just got to."

"Now, I'm not saying I don't earn my pay. I work hard, but I've worked hard at other places and never made deep into six figures like I do at Custom Accounting Designs. Plus," she added, "they have great benefits, pay top bonuses and nearly everybody at the company is super cool."

Gloria waved. "James and I heard about Custom Accounting Designs' Atlanta office from a friend. Other than what the friend told us, we don't know anything about the company. But we're always happy to help." She shrugged. "Glad it turned out to be a good fit."

Petula sat back on the seat. "Well. Thanks again."

"Do you work with people in Bensalem from your office in Atlanta?" Gloria asked.

"I do." Glancing out the window, Petula added, "But as much as I like Bensalem, I don't want to move back here." She shook her head. "I'm not one for revisiting the past unless it's with nostalgic conversation, old pictures or while talking with relatives I haven't seen in months while we're at a family reunion." She let out a deep sigh. "At the same time," she said, shaking her head, "I don't want to go back to the Atlanta office." She started rubbing her forehead, a slow back and forth across her forehead with the end of her fingers. "The thought of returning there is costing me sleep. If something's going on at the office, I don't want to know about it."

James and Gloria glanced at each other.

"What are you talking about?" Gloria asked. She laughed as if taking Petula's concern as a joke. "You sound like Custom Accounting Designs is into something shady."

"I don't think the company is into anything illegal," Petula said, looking at Gloria. "But that's not to say that everyone there is on the up-and-up."

"You're not going to get to the bottom of it hiding out up here," Gloria told her. "And I know you," she added. "You'll drown in concern until you face whatever is bothering you." She glanced at Petula, scanning the side of her face. "And I can tell that something's got you deep in thought."

Petula sighed, lowered then raised her head. "You're right. It's one of my shortcomings. I always try to figure things out. I always want to know what's really going on with something that's bothering me, and I always want to know what motivated a person to do wrong." Shaking her head in quick side to side motions, she said, "Been that way since I was a kid. Probably why I can spend hours watching true crime shows the rare times work is slow and I can rest weeknights and on weekends not needing to check emails or respond to a client's request."

She looked through the front windshield and said, "I haven't been sleeping good in weeks, even before I drove up here and ran into that Paul guy. Tossing and turning, trying to figure things out. Maybe I thought coming up here would make whatever's going on back in Atlanta go away." She snapped her fingers. "Like magic." She shook her head. "Just make everything turn right."

Gloria's brow rose. "Is it that bad at work, costing you sleep?"

"I hate to admit it—" Petula began, then she tried to change the subject, not wanting to deepen her apprehension. "Let's talk about something else," she said, waving her hand and working at a smile. "Going back there, even in my mind, is the last thing I want to do right now."

"Who are your friends at the company?"

Petula shrugged. "They don't work in the department I work in, so I don't see them much, but they're good people." She smiled. "There's a receptionist I'm cool with and two women in marketing."

"Maybe you should hang out with them more, could show you the good side of the job. Could make you feel that you're not facing whatever is going on at the firm alone," Gloria said.

Petula laughed. "Getting paid is the good side of the job on a lot of days lately. Plus, I wouldn't drag anyone else at the firm into whatever is going on."

Gloria twisted her mouth. "If you're that certain that something wrong is going on, why don't you go to authorities?"

"I don't have evidence that would hold up in court," Petula admitted. "Plus, I love the work I do. I really do love my job, and I think most of the employees there are good people. It's just Veronica." She shook her head. "She's been out to get me since we were at a regional meeting, and she overheard senior leadership bragging about my work. Then, she found out about my having lunch with one of her contacts." She didn't tell them that Veronica and she had once dated the same guy, howbeit months apart.

"Sounds like Veronica might be insecure," James chimed. "Might be time to extend her an olive branch. Who knows?" He shrugged. "She could turn out to be an ally, especially once she knows you're not competition."

"No," Petula answered flatly. "It wouldn't make sense for me to try to reconcile with her. She's the one who's had it in for me after she saw how much leadership respected my work. Plus, I think she's breaking company policies. I can't prove it, but I saw some things during the last audit. That's part of what's unnerving me. That's what I'm trying to forget."

"Isn't she the woman you used to brag about, telling us how much you admired her?" Gloria asked.

"Ye-Yes. When I first got to Atlanta, I was really impressed with Veronica. I mean. She's sharp and well connected. She knows powerful people, movers and shakers." Shrugging, she said, "But things are different now."

After a pause, Gloria asked, "Is Veronica used to being the star down there?"

Petula nodded. "She's an excellent program manager. People at the firm admire her. She's a go-getter. She's smart and very confident. She knows how to get people to do what she wants them to do, and she does it in a way where you'd never think that she was asking you for something." After a series of quick head nods, she added, "She knows how to get what she wants."

Gloria pulled in her bottom lip. "Do you think it's worth finding out if Veronica knows that Paul Gibbs guy?"

"Nah," Petula said, waving her hand. "She wouldn't go that far. She wouldn't do anything like that."

James looked into the rearview mirror at Petula. "You sure?"

Gloria turned up her nose and glanced over the headrest at Petula. "Sounds like Veronica's manipulative."

"She is."

"No wonder you don't like her," Gloria laughed. "You never did like anyone who played games. You're big on honesty and sincerity." She smiled. "That's what I like about you."

James looked into the rearview mirror. "Is Veronica at work now or is she on vacation too?"

"She's at work. We back each other up when one of us is out of the office. We can't be on vacation at the same time. There's a lot going on at the office. It's a busy time and for good reasons. We've gotten a lot of new clients, so we have a lot of work to do to onboard those clients. Our firm does more than just straight up insurance accounting work. We do presentations, educational seminars, budgeting training, tax audits, investments and a lot more. It's just all focused on helping clients grow their bottom line."

"Kind of like a quasi-financial services firm?" James asked.

"Not exactly," Petula said. "We don't do loans or anything like that."

"Does Veronica handle complex client accounts?" Gloria asked. "I mean, do you both see individual client taxes and other records and make changes or recommendations to those accounts?"

"Sometimes, but mainly we handle business and organizational accounts."

"Considering that you both handle complex individual accounts, even if you rarely do, maybe that's it," James said. "Think there could be a tie to what's happening to some of the accounts that you manage and what happened at the state forest and later at your hotel?"

Petula shook her head. "I don't even want to think like that." Shaking her head again, she was adamant. "There's no link to what happened to me here and the office. Custom Accounting Designs is a standup firm. We do way too many internal audits for any wrongdoing to go unnoticed for long. No way," she asserted. "There's no link. Plus, that Paul guy wouldn't know anyone from Custom Accounting Designs. There's no link," she repeated. "No way. No way." Image of the Custom Accounting Designs keychain dangling out of Paul's pant pocket at the forest flashed across her mind and she squinted, as if trying to erase the image.

"I know you don't think there's a reason to check who knows who, if anyone," Gloria said. "But it might be worth it, especially if you want to resolve what happened after you came up here."

"Oh, I'm going to dig," Petula said. "The facts will come out, but it has nothing to do with work. Plus, you know me and conflict. You know how much I dislike conflict and 'he said, she said'. You know that's not my thing." She released a long, breathy sigh. "But I will get to the bottom of what happened and why."

"Just be careful where you dig," Gloria said. "You don't want to step on the wrong toes."

"I won't be here when I do the deep digging," Petula revealed, sitting back on the seat and looking out the window.

James twisted his mouth. "I say you look through any accounts Veronica worked on that you also worked on that you think something suspicious could be happening with."

"Yes," Petula agreed. "I'll look into the accounts when I get back to your place."

"How are you going to do that?" Gloria asked. This time instead of looking through the front windshield, she glanced at James.

"I'll log in remotely."

"Okay. Good." Gloria said, looking at James. "If you tell us what you find, James and I might be able to help you get to the bottom of things."

"Thanks, but there's nothing you two can do. You don't know anything about what I do beyond the little I've told you," she said, certain that she must conduct the heart of the investigation, discovering what was going on, searching records, talking to the right people – alone -- despite how harrowing the situation might become. But first, she had to start digging for details.

## Chapter Eleven

Like the steady tick of a vintage grandfather clock echoing through an empty hall, Petula's gaze swept back and forth across the screen. Her eyes narrowed, disbelief curling into suspicion as the account audits flickered before her—numbers shifting just enough to make her question if something, or someone, was manipulating them.

"The numbers on about a dozen accounts aren't adding up." Sitting at Gloria's and James' round marble kitchen table, her laptop in front of her, she rubbed her forehead. "No way could the firm's top twelve clients have netted the same amount of return on their investments month after month for a quarter, let alone all of last year," she worried, her hand going across her brow. "And Reginald Lewis didn't resign as a partner at Service Leaders Retirement Fund. Why does this press release on file at Custom Accounting Designs say he did? Who wrote and distributed the release? Why would the company keep this?"

She leaned to within inches of the laptop monitor. "Who changed these numbers? They weren't here when I reviewed them a month ago, not like this. These numbers are crazy," she said out loud, looking over the top of her laptop screen at Gloria and James who sat in their living room on their modular L-sectional leather sofa, feet propped on the edge of their rectangular natural wood coffee table.

"I can't believe this," Petula moaned, turning partly away from the screen, not wanting to face what was there. "Way too many of these companies' profits are going into personal accounts and these clients' revenues are lower than they were when I did my audits. There's no reason to shield these clients from tax obligations." She shook her head. "It wasn't like this when I checked last month. It couldn't have been." Closing her eyes, she rested her head in her cupped hands. "No way could I have missed this. I mean," she frowned. Her mouth felt dry, like she'd been out in the heat too long. "I've had a lot on my mind, but I-I-I would have caught this."

"Damn it," she snapped, leaning back on the chair. "I've been making way too many mistakes, going to that forest, not charging my RV correctly and now seeing how I've screwed up at work." She looked at the table. "What's wrong with me?"

"You've been under a lot of stress," Gloria told her, waving her purple and gold polished, manicured fingernails. "Spend the rest of your time in Bensalem relaxing. You just need to chill. After you get some rest, you'll be your normal, sharp self," she smiled. "It'll all come back to you then."

"No," Petula said, volume in her voice rising. "No. No. No," she repeated, shaking her head. "No way should this be happening. On top of that, bills are being paid with new client fees. A novice wouldn't notice it, but I know these accounts. Damn." Leaning forward she said, "I know Custom Accounting Designs is a standup company. The firm is an industry leader, and I know I wouldn't set bills up to be paid from new client fees. I wouldn't do that," she said, begging the silence to make her words true. "I have to fix this."

Sinking down in the chair, she said, "It's got to be a computer glitch." Her shoulders rose, then lowered. "That's what it is. It's a computer glitch. As soon as I get back to work from vacation, our Atlanta team has got to inform the impacted clients." She sighed and looked into the living room where she saw Gloria and James now standing next to the sofa. "A computer glitch could explain some things." She peered at them. "But it won't explain everything." Facing her laptop screen, she said, "Who would do this?"

James pulled up on his faded Gatt jeans, leaned forward and stared into the kitchen, his glare hard on

Petula's forehead. "You said you've been under a lot of stress."

Petula looked across the room, gazing into space. "I know but I wouldn't mess up like this." She laughed, a noise meant to release pressure, not to express humor or gaiety. "I really am a rock-solid accountant and program manager."

"Would anybody think that you'd gain something if you did make a mistake?" James asked. "I mean, I know you would never do anything like that on purpose." He shrugged. "But, like you said, everybody makes mistakes."

"No," she answered. "I wouldn't take anything that didn't rightfully belong to me even if it did come from a mistake, I don't care who made the mistake." She looked at James. "I'm not that type of person. And I know you weren't saying I was." This time, she looked at Gloria. "But something's wrong with the numbers." Looking at James again, she added, "I don't know who stands to gain from this type of mistake. But that doesn't matter," she quickly added. "If this gets out, it could hurt Custom Accounting Designs. Damn," she cursed. "I hope I wasn't helping to mask any wrongdoing by not double-checking Veronica and the team that audits her work just because Veronica told me not to touch her records and even went so far as to encrypt files." She spun in a circle. "Why do I let Veronica bully me? Why don't I stand up to her more?"

"It won't help you to try to pin this on anyone," Gloria tried. When Petula met her glance, she continued, "Girl, you really need to find out what actually happened."

"I don't care who checks, I'm in the clear," Petula said, her voice shaky. "After Veronica told me to stay away from her files, I requested a special audit from outside regulators on several accounts. Anyone would know I wasn't trying to hide anything."

"What did the auditors say?" Gloria asked.

"I don't remember," Petula lied. She stood and closed her laptop, not bothering to log out of Custom Accounting Designs' employee portal, then she hurried, laptop in hand, and grabbed her keys and shoulder pocketbook off the counter. "I know I'm leaving early, but now that my RV is in the shop being repaired, I'm going to get ready to head back to Atlanta. Plus, I must return the car I rented earlier." She looked at Gloria and James, her face drawn down, eyes sorrowful. "I have no choice. I must head back."

When she reached the sofa, Gloria stepped in front of her. Placing her hands gently atop Petula's shoulders, she looked softly at her friend and said, "But all the stuff that went wrong happened here."

Shaking her head, Petula said, "I must get back."

Gloria stepped closer to Petula, the spark gone from her eyes. "We haven't gone to the boutique shops."

"I know," Petula sighed, pulling up on her laptop. "Promise we'll hang out more next time." Working at a smile, struggling to find one, she told Gloria, "I'll be up here again before you know it. But," she added, "No way can I act like what I saw in the records isn't a big deal. Clients deserve to know the truth and to have their records be correct."

Gloria examined Petula's face, the lines in her forehead, her tight brow. After she took in a deep breath, she told Petula, "Be careful."

Petula looked from Gloria to James back to Gloria. "Thanks so much for your help, but I really need to get going. My vacation might not have turned out the way that I wanted it to, but who knows how it all will turn out in the end." Shaking her head, she said, "Don't think I'm going to solve this from here. I really need to get back to Atlanta and dig through files to find out what's going on."

**\* \* \* \* \* \* \* \* \***

That's what she told Gloria and James, but she didn't go back to Atlanta. Instead, she went to Custom Accounting Designs' Bensalem office. Once there, she told the team that she was merely stopping in to finalize a project that she'd forgotten to complete before she started on vacation. Because of her solid reputation, no one at the Bensalem office questioned her.

"You can use this office at the back of the building. It's Mark's office. You know, Mark," Tonya, a unit executive assistant told her, leading Petula down a long hallway.

"Yes. I know Mark. He's the chief financial officer for the Northeast."

"Bingo," Tonya said. "He's on vacation this and next week, and he takes real vacations," she laughed.

"Thank you for letting me use the office," Petula nodded. "I won't be long."

"All you have to do is log in with your office credentials," Tonya said, leaning over a thin client computer placed on the top corner of the desk. "And wah-lah, you're in business."

"Smooth," Petula smiled. "Thanks again."

"Would you like me to close the door?"

"Please."

"You're such a dedicated worker," Tonya said, smiling softly at Petula. "Doing work on your vacation. I see announcements from the Atlanta office of you winning quarterly awards all the time."

"I do my best," Petula told her, glancing toward the door where Tonya now stood. "But let's keep it between us that I was here working. Arthur keeps telling me that I'll be in trouble if I don't start taking a *real* vacation," she laughed, hoping the gaiety would encourage Tonya to move along.

Tonya pulled on the door handle causing the door to close with a hush, at which time Petula hurried to log into her work portal. Her hands were unsteady when the portal opened, and she started, one calculated click after another, to access company files. She kept looking over her shoulder, checking to see if anyone was at the door. While records were uploading onto her laptop, she dug through old paper files in the desk side drawers, searching for details linked to the suspicious online accounts she'd come across while she'd been at Gloria's and James', certain her paper search would come up empty while, at the same time, she felt desperate for clues, evidence.

Then, she froze, staring at a familiar account name on a ledger in a paper file. Seconds later, her fingers rushed across the keyboard as she opened Custom Accounting Designs' intranet search browser and typed "Service Leaders Retirement Fund" into the search box. Instead of clicking on the half dozen articles that came up, she read the bold titles. "No way," she leaned forward and gasped, her gaze scanning the headlines, reading bits of the story summaries about Custom Accounting Designs helping military retirees finance a new home, pay for a college degree or start a business.

Her body fell back against the chair, images of Paul flashing like quick film shots across her mind. "What if Paul had something to do with this?" she whispered to the empty office. Seconds later, she rocked her head, dismissing the belief that Paul, a decorated military loner, had a significant connection to the company she worked for. What she couldn't do was erase the Custom Accounting Designs' keychain she'd seen Paul with the first day their paths had crossed.

She glanced at the clock in the laptop's bottom right corner. Then, realizing that time was not on her side, she leaned forward in the chair and returned to flipping through paper files, her fingers hurrying across the papers' top edges. As soon as she reached the last set of paper folders, she turned slowly, looking over her shoulder toward the office door.

"Knock. Knock," Tonya said, a tall plastic cup filled with water in her hand. "Brought you some water. Thirsty?" she asked when she reached Petula's side.

Slamming the desk drawer closed, Petula sat erect, ran her hand over the back of her hair and smiled. "Thank you, Tonya. You're so thoughtful. I appreciate it."

"I'll just put the cup here on the desk edge." She turned to walk away from Petula. "Is that okay?"

"Sure. And thanks again."

Sensing that she was alone again, Petula typed fast, her fingers racing across the keyboard as she searched for client accounts. Then, she leaned her chest across the desk edge.

"Finding everything okay?"

Petula's elbow bumped the cup of water, nearly knocking it over, when she turned and looked at the doorway. "Yes. Yes," she nodded at Tonya. "Just want to finish this project." When Tonya remained in the doorway, Petula said, "Do you mind closing the door?"

"Sure," Tonya obliged, putting her hand on the knob and pulling the door to a close. She looked at the shut door for a second, then turned and walked down the hallway.

"Hurry, Petula, hurry," Petula whispered to herself, hoping to calm her nerves. As fast as she moved, seconds felt like minutes to her. During her search, papers curled at the end; others fell out of her hands, splaying across the floor. At the end of her hunt through the paper files, she put her attention on the online accounts.

Twenty minutes into her search, she stared at the monitor. Her hand formed into a fist and was shaking. "Dale Stewart and Paul Gibbs are account holders for Abynix Computers, one of our key clients?" she whispered, glancing at the office door. "And Dale is listed as a voting officer for GYX Insurance." She stared at the screen. "What is going on?"

Her breath caught in her throat when she saw Dale's and Paul's names associated with a third firm, AI Enterprises Corporation. In sweeping glances, she sped through the names of the client board members, audit reports and accounting numbers.

"Oh, my goodness," she exclaimed, her heart racing, her mind struggling to believe what she was looking at. She fell back on the chair. Her hand was covering her mouth, working like a silencer, while she read the next names, "Gloria Blake, James Blake and Veronica Boyd." As if a ghost had entered the room, filling it with dread, she looked toward the door, then hurried and faced the window. Seconds passed before she faced the monitor again. "Gloria, James and Veronica are linked to three of the accounts," she whispered to herself, again glancing at the office door. "No," she begged. "No." She stared at the monitor for several seconds, tears pooling in her eyes, before she stammered, "Damn."

After she glanced over her shoulder at the door, she begged, "Lord, please don't let Gloria and James be part of this. That can't be why they encouraged me to transfer to the Atlanta office after I'd been in Atlanta a few months. That can't be why they were asking me about Veronica and the accounts, acting like they didn't know much about Custom Accounting Designs, trying to throw me off. No."

The only names she didn't see on the files were Officer Duggan's and Chris Eggers'. Absent another thought, she logged out of the portal, shoved two paper file folders between her laptop base and lid, then pressed the laptop tight against her hip and exited the office.

"Leaving so soon?" Tonya asked, peering over the top of her cubicle wall.

"Yes. Like I told you earlier, I knew I wouldn't be long. Plus, I have a personal appointment that I'm running late for," Petula told her, tightening her grip on her laptop, praying that the files wouldn't slide onto the floor. "It was good seeing you."

"Stop by again soon," Tonya said, standing and watching Petula hurry away from the office.

"Where is she going in such a hurry?" an account manager rounded a back corner, close to the office Petula had been sitting in, and asked Tonya.

"Said she had an appointment."

As soon as she stepped outside the office building, Petula started running. She ran to her rental car, passed a group of employees gossiping at the edge of the parking lot. Once inside the car, she placed the laptop on the passenger seat, fired up the engine and sped toward the Wellington Street police station.

Midday traffic was unusually light, for which Petula repeatedly said, "Thank you" as she made her way from the Custom Accounting Designs' Bensalem office to the police station. She was trembling when she leaned over the police station's front desk taking deep breaths. "Where's Officer Duggan?"

"He's in the back," a woman officer said, standing from a chair behind the desk. "May I ask what your name is?"

Pulling up on the laptop, Petula answered, "My name is Petula Abebe."

Raising a hand, the woman told her, "Wait just a second." Then, she went down a hallway.

When she returned to the front of the station, she was accompanied by Officer Duggan.

"How may I help you?" Officer Duggan asked, glancing at Petula's laptop.

"I need to show you something."

Officer Duggan opened the swinging gate that separated the visitor area from the area the police officers worked in. "Come on back."

While she followed him, Petula walked stealthily, as if she had committed a crime, her head slightly bowed, glancing at the woman police officer and other officers at the front of the station. The area, papers poking out unevenly from the tops of three-ring binders, and the lighting dim, felt dingy to her. When sunlight scraped its way inside the area and landed on a desk, Petula spotted dust; it lined much of the desktops, as if it was a dull paint coating.

Glancing at the tall metal filing cabinets behind the desks, Petula followed Officer Duggan inside a small interrogation room at the far back of the station. Once inside the room, settling into the familiarity of Officer Duggan's medium build and calm tenor voice, showing him the paper files, and online accounts she'd discovered, she leaned across the table and said, "I didn't have any other place to go."

"You did the right thing," he told her, scarcely looking up from the files.

Watching his gaze shift back and forth across the papers, she leaned further forward, "This is hard for me."

He didn't look up, flipping through the files as if he was alone in the room.

"Gloria and James have been friends of mine for years." Shaking her head, she said, "Even now, with everything I've seen in those files, it's hard to believe they have anything to do with this. They just can't be involved." She looked up at the wall, her gaze landing on a spider that dangled from the ceiling corner. "Thank goodness, our paths crossed." She was shaking her head again when she said, "I'd have to try to figure this out on my own if not for you."

With that, he paused. The smile he gave her was faint, the corners of his mouth only turning up slightly. "It's my job."

Recalling that his name wasn't in the files, she sighed into, "It's good to know there are still good people in this world, people you can count on, people you can trust."

"Yes." He sat back and looked right at her. "It's easy to cut corners and take advantage of someone. I always wanted to do the right thing." He shrugged. "Probably why I became a cop, but not even all cops do the right thing." He gave her a full smile, revealing a slight gap in his front teeth. "But I've always found that it's worked out best when you do the right thing." Chuckling, he told her, "Helps me sleep good at night too."

She leaned back in the chair, toying with her shirt collar. "What's going to happen next?"

"Keep this to yourself for now," he told her.

She paused for a long time, examining his face, the height of his shoulders, the pace of his breathing, checking to see if his hands were steady or shaking. "Okay," she finally said.

"You should be safe," he assured her as he walked her to the front of the station. After he opened the station's exit door, he told her, "I'll be in touch. Stay in town until you hear from me."

She clutched her laptop. "But why?"

"I'm working on something with the FBI involving what you showed me."

She stared at him in disbelief.

"Can't go into details," he told her. "The firm could be helping some bad actors run a shell scheme. That's all I can tell you right now."

She laughed, a dry cackle. "That's all you're going to tell me? After all I've been through," she added, stepping back. "You're not going to give me more details on what's going on?"

"Let's just say I'm not sure how much you trust your friends."

She nodded. "Fair enough. But I won't tell them anything," she promised even as years of friendship she'd shared with Gloria and James pinched the promise with uncertainty that she'd keep it. Recalling the accounts that she'd seen Gloria's and James' names on, she turned away from Officer Duggan, her pulse throbbing as she swallowed hard and fought back a hot surge of tears.

## Chapter Twelve

The next two days were uneventful, slow, mundane and predictable, for Petula. To avoid Gloria and James, she stayed at a hotel in Princeton, New Jersey, rarely venturing outside except to get healthy snacks from a nearby grocery store. It was noon, a partly cloudy ordinary day. She was standing in front of her hotel room's large bay window when her cellphone rang.

Seeing South Doyle Police Department on the screen, she picked up the call. "Hello?"

"Petula Abebe?"

"Officer Duggan?"

"Yes. Is this Petula?"

"It is."

"You haven't spoken with Gloria or James, correct?"

"No, I haven't. I stayed in town and laid low, just like you requested. Returned my rental car this morning. Still don't know why you wanted me to stay here."

"It was in case we needed you to get information from Gloria and James."

"Oh," she laughed, her jaw tight. "Using me for a safety net."

"It's a dirty game."

"Promise me that you will find out how involved Gloria and James are," Petula asked, her lip tremoring. "Gloria was a good friend for years. We roomed together one year in college." Shaking her head, she said, "She just wouldn't do this. She's responsible. She's kind. She's honest." She paused, searching the room for answers. "Maybe James and she were in a financial bind. Maybe someone threatened Gloria. Maybe she didn't really know what was going on." She turned in a half circle, as if trying to avoid facing her friends' involvement in the crime. Then, she pressed her cellphone against her ear. "No way would Gloria just do this. There's got to be more to it."

"We'll definitely keep investigating what happened, but I can't make promises."

"I see." She paused; not sure she believed him. "What now?"

"Head back to your home in Sandy Springs just outside of Atlanta. Lay low. Don't go into the office. Just go home and wait to hear from me."

"Why didn't you tell me about this earlier?"

He was quick. "I couldn't."

She released a deep breath before she asked, "Who are the FBI agents you're working with?"

"You wouldn't know them."

"Maybe not. But what are their names?"

"Agent Keisha Stamps and Agent Marco Tai. They're both based out of Atlanta."

"They work in Buckhead?"

"No. They work in downtown Atlanta."

"All right," she sighed, rolling her eyes. "To Atlanta it is." In the back of her mind, she made a note to research Agent Keisha Stamps and Agent Marco Tai and, as much as she didn't want to, Officer Monroe Duggan.

"Petula, thank you for what you're doing."

"Sure," she said, her hands curling, then cupping, forming into fists. "Wish you would have told me what was going on right from the start."

"Like I told you before, I couldn't. By now, you should know that."

"I was in danger," she fumed. Images of being chased by Paul and his dogs, her breath thick and taxing in her lungs as she raced toward the river, desperate for the murky water to serve as a veil, surfaced in her mind. Looking toward the hotel room window, she scowled and screamed, "I could have been killed."

"Look," he began. "I had no definitive confirmation about your identity or that you knew Gloria and James as well as you do until you came into the police station with those files, telling me what you did."

"Guess I have no choice but to believe you. I know so little about all of this." She glared across the room, her brow furrowed. "I'm being kept in the dark."

"I know it's not easy. These cases are never easy. But just go home to Atlanta, stay out of the office, and lay low until you hear from me."

"Okay," she nodded, resigning to the fact that, for now, her life didn't seem to belong to her if she wanted to get to the bottom of the disturbing happenings that had occurred over the past few days and free herself of the haunting accounting findings.

Moments later, she was on the telephone with a representative at the RV repair shop in Cranberry, a small town on the outskirts of Princeton. "Sure. Thank you," she said, speaking in small bites, as if in a hurry. "I'll be there in half an hour," she told the representative while she scribbled the address to the repair shop on a hotel notepad.

She ended the call. Then, she pulled up her Uber app. "Please pick me up at 0444 Main Street, Princeton, NJ."

Seconds later, she smiled when she looked at the app and saw that there was a driver in the area who would pick her up in less than ten minutes.


The Uber ride from the hotel in Princeton to the RV repair shop in Cranberry took less than forty minutes.

"Will you stay here until I get my RV?" Petula asked the Uber driver after she got out of the Sonata.

The driver nodded, "Sure."

It was a short walk from the parking lot to the repair shop office. A man held the shop door open for her as if he'd been expecting her.

"Thank you," she told the man, happy to finally be getting her RV back in working order. She entered the shop, pulling in her stomach and moving beyond the man who continued to stand at the door. Hope about getting her own wheels back lifted her spirits; soon she was smiling. She nearly tossed her head back and sighed when the repair shop clerk returned her RV keys and said, "If you'll just sign here, you'll be set."

One glance at the repair bill and Petula groaned, "Ouch."

Not the one responsible for paying the bill, the clerk laughed.

Petula glanced at the laughing clerk, then gawked at the bill. "Fifteen hundred dollars."

"Your warranty covers the work," the clerk told her.

"Thank Goodness," Petula said, shaking her head. She tsked while she waited for the clerk to work up her receipt.

"Your RV is right outside those doors," the clerk said, pointing to her left. "It's on the first row. You can't miss it."

"Thank you," Petula nodded.

"And it's running and purring like a kitten," the clerk smiled as she watched Petula fold her copy of the bill and receipt. "Oh, and another thing."

"Yes?" Petula asked, turning and facing the clerk again.

"The maintenance technician found this on the side of your RV," she said, holding up a small black box. "It was inside the frame rail. It's a tracker."

Petula approached the clerk and opened her palm. "Thank you." She turned the tracker in her hand. "Do you know where it was made?" Raising her eyebrows, she asked, "Can you tell?"

The clerk shook her head. "No. These things are made and sold practically everywhere these days. But," she said, raising a finger, "where were you when you last had your RV serviced?"

Rubbing her chin, Petula retraced the last two weeks of her life. "I was in Atlanta. Come to think of it," she said, "I had it serviced before I hit the road, nothing major, just regular servicing."

"Well," the clerk said, twisting her mouth, "that might be a good place to start."

"Sure," Petula nodded. She started walking toward the exit door, then stopped and turned. She was leaning over the counter the clerk sat behind when she asked, "How many people can know a person's whereabouts if one of these trackers is attached to their vehicle?"

"A technician would probably know better than me, but with a really good computer system, an experienced computer tech or a good hacker could get the whereabouts to a dozen or more people easily."

"Thank you," Petula nodded. Then, she turned and exited the repair shop. Seconds later, she hurried back inside the shop. Digging through her shoulder pocketbook, she pulled out the cellphone tracker and handed it to the clerk asking, "Ever seen one of these?"

Giving Petula a once over, one eyebrow higher than the other, the clerk answered, "It looks like a cellphone tracker." She backed away from Petula. "Are you okay?"

"Ye-Yes," Petula stammered, wishing she had remembered the cellphone tracker sooner, while she'd had the rental car. If she had, she knew she would have given the tracker to Officer Duggan.

The clerk twisted her mouth and nodded.

"I-I really am okay," Petula repeated, working to put the clerk at ease. "Thanks for your help." On her way out the door, she dropped the cellphone tracker inside her shoulder pocketbook, promising herself that she'd stop at a technology service center before she entered the interstate to Atlanta.

As she prepared to exit the RV repair shop parking lot, she pulled her RV next to the Uber driver's Sonata, tipped and thanked the driver, then, her hands firm on the RV steering wheel, she headed for a technology service center at a major computer retailer located in a nearby strip mall.

"Is there a way to track where this device came from and how long it's been in use?" Petula asked the first technician who approached the counter. As she watched the technician examine the device, she kept wondering why anyone would put a tracker on her RV and on her cellphone.

Then, looking at the technician, she wondered if whoever had put the portable tracker on her cellphone knew that her RV was in the shop and, to stay aware of her whereabouts, the person had attached the device to the back of her phone. A bounty of questions filled her mind, including where she'd been when the tracker was put on her cellphone. "How could I have missed that someone had picked up my phone?" she worried, staring at the tracker, feeling exposed, her privacy stolen. "Am I in danger?"

Chapter Thirteen

Turning the tracker in her hand, examining its smooth, round shape, the technician peered up at Petula. "Looks like a Montrey 1211. It's a newer model mini tracker. It's waterproof and," she added, turning the tracker over, "It can pick up audio."

Surprise mixed with disbelief then fear, caused Petula to step back and stammer, "Are you saying whoever put that on my phone might have been listening to my conversations?"

Before she responded, the technician looked across the counter at Petula's cellphone. "Your cellphone has topnotch privacy and security features." Turning the tracker in her hand, she added, "The tracker might not have been able to pick up audio on your phone." She nodded into, "Your phone is so secure, it's probably why whoever wanted to know your whereabouts used a physical device. I don't know of a tracking app that could access your phone without your awareness. But this," she said, squeezing the portable device, "it could keep track of you."

"Who?" Petula muttered, "would want to keep up with my whereabouts to the point of putting this tracker on my phone?" After a pause, she offered, "The only person who might have put the tracker on my cellphone is this guy I ran into when I first came to the area. I was at the Whooten State Forest," she added, shaking her head. "But he's been picked up and he never got close enough to me to put a tracker on my cellphone." Burying her head in her hand, she searched her mind, digging through the past for anyone who could be desperate to keep up with her. Her emotions rocked from confusion to anger to dread. "I don't know who would do this," she finally looked up and told the technician. "How can I make sure it's turned off?"

"You could break it," the technician laughed.

"No," Petula said, pursing her lips. "I don't want to break it. I want to find out who put it on my cellphone. I want to use it as evidence."

The technician laughed again. "Jealous boyfriend?"

"Nah."

"Well, to be safe, reset your cellphone to the factory settings, disable your phone's location and leave this device away from your phone."

"Thanks," Petula nodded, confusion building within her, taking the tracker from the technician and heading toward the store's exit door, determined to find out who put the tracker on her phone.

Sunrays brushed across her face when she stepped outside. Having skipped breakfast, on her way to her RV, she spotted a deli -- pictures of sandwiches, macaroni salad, chips and veggies taped to the bottom of the front window -- at the opposite end of the strip mall. It was a short walk from the technology service center to the deli where she ordered a smoked turkey, lettuce, tomato and pickle wrap and a bottle of water.

When she returned to her rig, she placed the bottled water in the RV's front cup holder. Most of the turkey wrap she ate while she sat in the RV's driver's seat, watching shoppers pulling in and out of parking spots and entering different stores at the strip mall.

Moments later, her stomach full and nerves settling, she slipped the RV into drive and eased out of the lot. A left turn took her onto a narrow two-lane road that stretched out before her, unfamiliar and long, as if the road had no end. As she curved around a jug handle, something tugged at her intuition. Glancing into the rearview mirror, her breath caught—far behind, scarcely visible through the passing traffic, a white van emerged from the bend.

"It's not Paul," she told herself, her pulse quickening as she glanced into the rearview mirror. When she looked forward, her gaze landed on a woman driving a green SUV with a kid playing with plastic cartoon characters in the back seat. As the woman and kid passed her, going in the opposite direction, Petula rolled her eyes. "I've got to stop thinking everyone in a white van is dangerous." A second later, she glanced into the rearview mirror.

On both sides of the road were trees and grass, mostly grass. She drove at a steady pace, but she couldn't stop looking into the rearview mirror, eyeballing the van, wondering why it was still behind her. "Paul's in jail," she reminded herself, putting more weight on the accelerator.

The next time she glanced into the rearview mirror, the van seemed to be speeding up, closing in on her. The quarter mile separating her and the van had become about two hundred yards, half its former distance.

Thinking that she could lose the van or at least determine if the driver was indeed following her, she took the first right. Her hands were gripping the steering wheel four sharp turns later when she looked up and saw the van yet trailing her.

She drove past a series of stores, then made the decision to enter a business center that was sandwiched between a gym and a dentist's office. Bringing her RV to a screeching stop -- parking so wildly the rig took up two lanes -- she ran inside the business center, hurrying up to a security guard. While she spoke with the guard, she kept glancing out the business center's windows.

"A guy in a white van is chasing me," she told the guard, her fingers hurrying across her phone's front panel, dialing 911. "I'm calling the police," she told the guard.

Several minutes passed before she took a deep breath. Her heart continued to race, feeling as if it was thumping against her chest. "They said they're sending a police cruiser by. Fortunately, they think there's a cruiser in the area." She looked at the guard, eager to flee the area, escaping the van. "Do you mind coming outside until I get on the road if the cop doesn't arrive soon?" she asked, unwilling to stick around and chance the police letting the van driver leave the area after questioning him, putting her at greater risk of being followed home.

It surprised her when the guard agreed, following her outside. The closer they got to her RV, the easier it was for her to spot the van and make out Paul sitting behind the driver's steering wheel, the bruise a lighter red yet still on his forehead.

"Is that your rig?" the security guard asked Petula.

"Yes."

"Tell you what. If the cops aren't here in the next three seconds, you get in your rig and pull off. I'll go talk with the van driver, giving you a chance to get away." Showing her his cellphone, he said, "I've already taken a picture of the guy in the van for when the cops show up. Plus, the business center's CCTV has most likely caught him and his van on video."

"When the cops arrive, please give them the van's plate number," she told him, stepping off the sidewalk, determined to make it to Interstate 95 before Paul left the parking lot.

At the same time, she stepped off the sidewalk, Paul drove his van forward, the front end dented, as if a witness to his efforts to ram the vehicle through Chris' front door less than a week ago.

Waving his hands and stepping in front of the van, the security guard approached Paul's vehicle. Before Paul punched the accelerator, a police cruiser pulled inside the strip mall, nearing the back of the van.

Petula watched the security guard wave down the cop then she ran to her RV, her stride getting wider with each step. Unlocking the rig and snatching the door open, she climbed inside and started the engine.

"This guy was harassing a woman to the point that she'd run inside the business center," she overheard the security guard tell the cop. "If you detain the van driver and come inside, I can pull up security video to show you what happened." Glancing at Petula, the security guard added, "The woman was so scared, she ran inside, called 911 and left."

"Thank you," Petula mouthed to the security guard as she pulled her RV toward the parking lot exit. Three turns and one mile later, she was speeding onto Interstate 95, heading toward Atlanta realizing that Paul must have been released from jail a few days after Officer Duggan had him escorted to the police station, angry that no one, not even Officer Duggan, had contacted her to notify her of Paul's release.

She was pushing 80 miles per hour, thirty minutes away from Cranberry, New Jersey when she started squeezing then releasing the steering wheel, trying to calm her nerves. Before she knew it, she was driving with one hand and digging through her shoulder pocketbook with the other hand. She didn't stop digging through the pocketbook until she had the cellphone tracker in her hand at which time she rolled down the window and tossed the tracker outside, hurling it against the pavement.

Fourteen hours later, she pulled into her townhome driveway in Sandy Springs, Georgia, relieved that she'd not seen one white van the entire time she'd been on Interstate 95. When she turned off the ignition, she folded her arms, leaned over the steering wheel and released several deep breaths.

"Thank you, Lord," she gasped, rolling her hands back and forth across the steering wheel. "It feels so good to be home." Although she was hundreds of miles from Doylestown and the Whooten State Forest, she kept looking over her shoulder after she took hold of her suitcase handle, laptop case and the two shopping bags that she'd gotten during her Franklin Mills Mall visit and brought them inside her townhouse.

A moment later, the front door closed and locked, the comforts of home tucked her inside a cocoon of safety. For the first time in over two weeks, when she called Ariana later that afternoon, she stayed on the phone with her for more than an hour, chatting about family, sports and goings on in Ohio, namely Columbus and Dayton. Not once did she mention Officer Duggan, Paul or the accounts at work.

"So happy that you're home and your RV is running like a pearl again," Ariana said at the end of their call.

"Me too."

"Ready to get back to work?"

Petula laughed. "Not exactly. Feel like I could use another week of vacation."

"How were the boutique shops? Catch any great deals?"

"Didn't get to Newtown. Hung out in Bensalem and Princeton." She stared at an abstract painting on her dining room wall. "It was just nice to be away."

"Well, maybe we'll get to the boutique shops together later this year. Mara and Paula would like to hang out at the shops, and you know how much they adore their Aunt Petula." Shaking her head, she added, "Phew, shopping. Those girls are becoming fashionistas and they're still young."

Petula smiled. "I'd like to get to Newtown with you and my two super cool nieces."

"Yes," Ariana nodded. "And I know what you mean about wanting another week off from work. I'm going to take a few days off next month, hang out with Leon and the girls. I need the break," she sighed. "Even with the meds, my blood pressure has been in the 170s again."

"Get some rest," Petula advised, lowering then rubbing her forehead. "Take care of yourself and when you get away from work, make sure you take a real vacation, not the kind I just had."

"I thought you had fun?"

"It was better than being at work, but it could have been more relaxing." Sighing, she looked toward the ceiling and rolled her eyes. "Think I'll lay low this weekend to catch up on rest before I head back to the office on Monday."

"There you go," Ariana smiled. "Treat yourself right."

"Yes. Always good talking to you, Ariana. I'll call you in a few days and," she added, "stop worrying. Take care of yourself so you can get your pressure in a safe range."

"I will," Ariana sighed.

"All right. Have a good one."

"You too. Love you, Sis."

By nightfall, the sharp fear of having been stalked at the state forest and later, in Doylestown and Cranberry, began to escape her, exhaustion replacing dread. She slept well, deeply, that night.

A day later, while she busied herself in her backyard garden, watering petunias, Officer Duggan called. Pulling her cellphone out of her pant pocket, she asked, "When does this end?"

Ignoring her question, he asked, "Are you home?"

"Yes."

"Meet me at the Pleasantry Café on Roswell Road."

She frowned at his insistence. "What time? And," the sound of Officer Duggan's voice nudging her memory, "why didn't you tell me that Paul had been released?" Before he had a chance to answer, she added, "He followed me after I picked up my RV and there was a tracker on my cellphone," she frowned. "I'm lucky I saw the tracker. It was hidden behind the protective cover I keep on the back of my cellphone."

"Sorry about Paul. I asked the clerk at the jail to contact me as soon as Paul was released---"

"--Your team isn't so sharp," she snapped.

"People make mistakes," he told her.

"This mistake could have cost me my life." She clenched her teeth. "I don't know what he would have done to me. What," she screamed, "was I supposed to do, call the police station or jail every single day, checking to see if Paul was still being held? I thought I was safe from him after you picked him up," she murmured.

She sat in silence, filling with anger, yet determined to put the entire situation behind her, she finally blurted, "What time should I meet you?" She gazed at a flock of swallows as they made their way across the sky, shaking her head, tightening her jaw.

"In fifteen minutes."

"Are you already there?"

"Yes," he told her.

"How long have you been at the café?"

"Just got here. Don't rush. Last thing we need is for you to get in an accident. We really need your help to win this case."

She drove her black and red Ford Mustang to the café, rubbing her forehead with the edge of her right hand, pondering the fact that police officers weren't authorized to work cases outside their state lines. Along the way, she thought about stopping at a convenience store and buying a protein bar and a bottle of water so she wouldn't feel hungry at the café, allowing her to get in and out of the establishment within minutes. Lingering in conversation with Officer Duggan didn't appeal to her.

**\*\*\*\*\*\*\*\*\*\***

The protein bar wrapper was balled and stuffed in her pant pocket when she leaned toward Officer Duggan at the café and asked, "You really want me to go into the office today and act like nothing's going on?" Rolling her eyes, she said, "It's Friday, the last day of my vacation."

He bit into the last piece of his cherry pastry. "Yes," he told her between chews. "It's important that you act normal. Come up with a reason to go in early. Are you working on a project?"

"Not a project that's so important I need to cut my vacation short." She grimaced. "If I go in the office today, I'll be going in a day before my vacation ends. People will be suspicious."

Licking the sugary icing off his fingers, he told her, "No they won't. You work there, and you already said you went into work at the Bensalem office."

"That's different and you know it."

His brow tightened. He leaned close to her, brushing her face with his breath. "Go into the office today."

Her mouth swung open.

Before she could speak, he said, "We have to take that chance."

"How long has this so-called shell scheme been going on?

"At least three years. The first two and a half years, they were smart. They started slowly, then they got greedy and started making mistakes. They might have gotten away with the scheme for several more years if they hadn't gotten greedy."

Petula rocked forward then slammed her back against the chair cushion. Shaking her head, she begged, "How is this even allowed to happen?"

"Fake resignation letters of prominent business leaders, stock market pump and dumps, bogus boards, fraudulent audits, the list goes on."

Petula stared across the restaurant, her face blank, her thoughts confused, jumbled.

A waiter passed their table, and Officer Duggan raised his hand, calling out, "Check, please."

Petula stood while Officer Duggan paid the bill, a green tea being her only item on the tab.

Officer Duggan tipped the waiter ten dollars then Petula and he exited the café. They were standing on the café's front walkway when Petula said, "If it'll get all of this madness out of my life, I'm heading to the office now." Gritting her teeth, she told him, "I just want this to be over."

"Meet me at Stewart's Deli in Buckhead two hours from now."

Petula closed her eyes before she said, "Got it." Her mouth was tight.

Halfway to her car, she stopped. "Officer Duggan, will I be safe at the office?"

Seconds passed before he said, "You're smart. If you keep your wits, you should be okay." Then, he added, stepping away from her, "I'm just a phone call away if you ne-ed anything."

Chapter Fourteen

    All lanes of Atlanta's Highway 400 were jammed, vehicles sandwiched together bumper-to-bumper, drivers' frustration building. Amid the congestion, like a wingless bird trapped in a cage, was Petula.

    Little by little Petula moved forward, one slow, deliberate tire rotation after another. An hour passed before she pulled inside the parking lot at Custom Accounting Designs. She sat in her parked car, seat reclined so no one across the lot could see her. "You can do this. You can do this," she repeated to herself for several seconds before she pulled her seat up, inhaled a deep breath and opened her car door.

    "What are you doing back today?" Lakeisha, the office receptionist, asked as soon as Petula entered the lobby.

    "Can you believe I got all the way to Philadelphia before I realized I had to finish an audit." She tossed her hand into the air and rolled her eyes. "Critical regulatory deadlines. Can't be late."

    "You are so invested in this place," Lakeisha laughed, rolling her wheelchair to the curved reception desk entrance. "No way would I have come in. You were up near the Bensalem office. You should have just finished the work there."

"Yes, but I didn't have the files and forms I need to complete the audit." Mimicking Lakeisha, hoping that it would give her an out, Petula laughed. "Like you said, who wants to work on vacation? I wasn't hardly thinking about an audit and taking documents with me when I left."

"I'm with you on that," Lakeisha smiled. "Hopefully, you don't have to stay long," she added, craning her neck and watching Petula make her way to the elevators. "And hey, if you're looking for Arthur or any of the senior leaders," she shouted at Petula's moving back, "they're in a meeting."

As soon as she stepped on the elevator and the silver doors closed, Petula shut her eyes and took deep breaths, working to steady her nerves. When the elevator doors opened, she leaned forward and looked down one end of the hallway then the other.

"Thank, Goodness," she whispered when she saw the hallway empty, swiveling her head from side to side, searching for onlookers. Seeing no one, she closed her eyes and massaged her forehead. Hurrying down the hallway in the direction of the Jacob Moore painting that hung on the back wall, she sped toward Veronica's office.

The door was open, so she peered inside. When she saw that the office was empty, she glanced over her shoulder, again inspecting the hallway. Seeing no one, she entered the office, moving quietly yet quickly. She hurried across the floor to a large metal filing cabinet, the same cabinet she'd found her client's signature file inside months ago. As soon as she reached the cabinet, she opened the top drawer and started shuffling through the papers so fast, the sharp end of the papers cut her hand. Stepping back, she saw spots of her blood on the papers. "Gotta take these too," she whispered to herself, laying the papers inside folders on top of the cabinet, leaving a second blood trail when she grabbed the papers and blood droplets landed at the bottom of two papers she failed to take.

Less than five minutes later, three manilla folders were tucked against her chest when she exited Veronica's office, her shin bumping a wastebasket at the door, turning it sideways. Looking down the long hallway and still seeing no one, she went straight into her office, shut the door and pulled the blinds partway closed.

She turned her laptop screen toward the window, hoping to prevent anyone who might enter her office from seeing what was on the screen. Then, she pulled out the client records she'd grabbed out of Veronica's office and rushed to scan and save them on a flash drive.

As soon as she heard Arthur's voice, its deep, smooth and confident tone, she froze. Too scared to move, anxious with uncertainty and guilt, she listened while Arthur beckoned his executive assistant, "Brenda, please call housekeeping and ask them to clean this conference room. We're almost done in here and I'd like the leftovers, plates and cups taken out."

From the sound of Arthur's voice, Petula knew that he was in the smaller conference room six doors away from her office. Checking her cellphone, she saw that it was one-twenty in the afternoon. A hard lump formed in her throat as she watched Veronica's scanned files download onto the flash drive.

This time when she glanced at the door, her gaze landed on the heavy glass fifth year service anniversary plaque Arthur had awarded her two years ago. "So proud of you," he'd told her just before he gave her a warm embrace at the anniversary dinner he'd put together in her honor. "You've done so much for the firm. We wouldn't be where we are now without you," he'd added, patting her back.

The sight of the plaque, its thick premium glass curved, its beautiful engraving highlighting her name, triggered memories for Petula. If not for Arthur, her paycheck wouldn't be topping $5,600 a week. She couldn't afford to live at her luxury Sandy Springs townhouse. The money to afford to purchase and maintain the upkeep of her RV would be out of her reach.

As she watched the files download on the flash drive, she considered snatching the flash drive out of the thin client. "After all," she mused to herself, "Officer Duggan has no idea what's happening here right now. He'll never know if I was able to retrieve documents that would implicate Custom Accounting Designs of engaging in illegal business practices."

Her head was buried in her hands, her shoulders tight with sorrow and regret. She thought about pulling Arthur aside, telling him what might be going on at the company, and making it clear to Arthur that she would do whatever it took to clear Custom Accounting Designs' name, protecting the firm's brand, giving leadership the opportunity to rectify potential wrongs without the public knowing about the transgressions.

The next instant, Paul's image and the altered files she'd discovered while at Gloria's and James' home popped into her mind, thrusting Arthur's kindness toward her into the background and, staring at the flash drive, she prayed for the files to hurry and finish downloading. While the last digital files were downloaded, she focused her attention on unscanned paper files stored in her office desk drawers.

Turning away from the thin client and the award plaque, the first paper file she grabbed out of her side desk drawer slipped out of her grasp, falling to the floor, papers splattering around her feet and chair. "Damn," she cursed, leaning over and picking the papers up. Without looking closely at the wording or accounting numbers on the papers, she scanned the files onto the flash drive, hoping she'd gotten the right files, too scared to double check herself.

"Damn it," she swore moments later when the scanner on the end of her desk jammed.

Hearing footsteps in the hallway, she looked over her shoulder, her heart racing. While the last dozen documents were downloaded onto the flash drive, she stood and walked to the door.

She peered into the empty hallway. It offered her no comfort as she was certain that she'd heard someone walk by then stop outside her office door.

The hallway didn't remain empty long as a tall shadow filled the doorway. "Surprised to see you here," a familiar voice said seconds before Petula downloaded the last file onto the flash drive.

Petula spun around in her chair, facing the door. "Veronica."

Veronica crossed her arms and leaned against the door's hinge, her brow furrowed, "Why are you here today?"

"Remembered that I had to finish something, so I decided to come into the office. Getting ready to leave though," she smiled at Veronica, her voice jerky. "I do have the rest of the day to enjoy my vacation." She told herself to breathe, then she asked, "How long have you been standing there?"

Chuckling, Veronica said, "A few seconds." She raised her crossed arms. "And just how was your vacation?"

"Actually, it was quite pleasant," Petula smiled as she placed her laptop in her laptop bag, Veronica's paper files inside the laptop between the monitor and keyboard, then headed for the door. She held Veronica's gaze while she slipped the flash drive inside her pant pocket.

"Just make sure you're in the office on time on Monday," Veronica smirked. "Just because you came in for a few minutes today doesn't mean you can come in late Monday."

"Yeah. Yeah. Yeah," Petula said, waving her hand in the air. She wanted to run to the elevators, but didn't, walking in long, hurried strides instead.

Her chest felt tight, heavy, by the time she reached the main building lobby. "Have a good one," she told Lakeisha as she walked through the lobby, glancing away from a security camera in a top ceiling corner.

"You too," Lakeisha said.

Before Lakeisha was able to say another word, Petula was in the parking lot, running toward her car. For just a second, she sat in her Mustang breathing with her eyes closed. Then, she pinched her upper thigh, searching for the flash drive. Certain that the flash drive was still in her pocket, not fallen on the lobby floor, she turned on the ignition and drove three blocks to Stewart's Deli.

"Who is this?" she asked, looking at an ebony skinned man with a short afro, while she stood at the edge of the table Officer Duggan sat at in Stewart's Deli.

Officer Duggan stood. "Petula, this is Agent Nick Mason." Turning to the agent, he said, "Agent Mason this is Petula Abebe. She's been helping me with the shell scheme case. She stumbled onto the case by accident, while vacationing in New Jersey and Pennsylvania."

Agent Mason stood then quickly sat again. "Were you able to scan and download the files onto the flash drive?"

"Where are agents Keisha Stamps and Marco Tai?" Petula demanded, looking from Agent Mason to Officer Duggan.

"They're busy with another case right now," Agent Mason told her. He had a thick, rubbery neck and a wide muscular frame, the type of brawny frame that intimated people.

It took her a long time to swallow the change, absorb another unexpected shift that had a direct impact on her but that she was last to become aware of. She clenched her teeth, nodded then, slowly lowering onto the bench, sat next to Agent Mason, across from Officer Duggan.

Agent Mason held out his hand, waiting for her to drop the flash drive inside his palm.

"I have a copy of everything that's on this flash drive," she told him. "So, you better be on the up and up, and I mean it or you'll both be implicated too," she added, looking at Officer Duggan.

"Fair enough," Agent Mason told her. "You're free to go home. Or you can drive back to the office if you want to watch some of your colleagues being escorted out of the building."

She gasped as her hands spread across the table, nearly knocking over Agent Mason's glass of sweetened tea, shocked at the coldness in his request. "You're going to arrest them today?"

Chapter Fifteen

Agent Mason scanned the deli's customers then frowned at her. "Lower your voice."

"No," she scowled. "I don't want to see anyone arrested." Her shoulders caved when images of Gloria and James flashed across her mind, filling her with stabbing regret and a sorrow that was beginning to morph into painful mourning. "What's going to happen to Gloria and James back in Bensalem?"

"We can't release that information," Agent Mason told her.

"Are they safe?"

"Yes."

"What if they didn't know what was going on?" Petula stammered. "What if they're innocent, victims themselves?"

"Don't worry about them," Agent Mason told her. "And don't contact them."

Less than five minutes later, she found herself sitting at the wheel of her Mustang. She intended to drive home, pretend that she hadn't just worked to implicate her colleagues, but for a reason she didn't understand, she made a U-turn at the end of the street and drove back to the office.

From where she sat in her car at the edge of the office parking lot, she felt like a spectator, eagerly curious, an innocent bystander watching the end of a bitter conflict in a Shakespeare play. Several minutes passed, her gaze shifting across the lot that was vacant of human traffic, filled only with parked cars, trucks and SUVs. Then, everything changed.

She found herself swallowing hard, biting back raw emotion, choking back tears. A looming guilt swooped in on her, growing in strength until it felt like it was choking her. As many run-ins and disagreements as she'd had with Veronica over the years, culpability stabbed at her conscience when she sat in her car at the far edge of the office parking lot and watched Veronica and Arthur being led away from the building, their heads bowed, agents trailing them.

"Never be a rat," she recalled her father and uncle telling her when she was a kid. It was a neighborhood motto – you did not tell on people. As much as she hadn't started the investigation, she knew she had turned the files over to Officer Duggan. She grimaced and knew that, as hard as she tried, she couldn't convince herself that she had no part in what she was witnessing from the safety of her vehicle.

The closer they got to the two police cars parked at the building's front edge, the longer Petula fixed her gaze on Arthur, and the tighter the lump in her throat felt. She watched an officer lower Arthur's head below the hood, ushering him inside the police cruiser.

A tear went slow and hot down her face. She felt completely alone sitting in her car, as if she was unworthy of anyone's trust, like she'd made a wrong turn somewhere in her life, an error that had pushed her toward this moment.

Her cellphone buzzed several times before she picked it up. "Hello?"

"This is Officer Duggan."

"Yes."

"Sorry you had to see that."

"Arthur hired me at the Atlanta office," she told Officer Duggan. "He was one of my biggest supporters. Sure. He supported Veronica too, but he never did me wrong. I just can't believe," she said, shaking her head, "that Arthur was in on this."

"They ran a clean shell game."

Petula tossed her head back, resting it on the seat cushion. Then, in a long, slow curve, she leaned forward. "I could have gone home, but for some reason, I didn't. I came back here." She shrugged. "Don't know why."

"Meet me at Pleasantry Café on Roswell Road, where we met earlier today."

"Why? I've run in enough circles for you today, don't you think?"

"I want to give you closure and thank you for your help." He paused. "You deserve that."

A large orangish, brown sparrow flew in front of her windshield. She stared at the bird, watching it flap its wings for several seconds, wiping away tears, before she told Officer Duggan, "I'm headed that way now."

"Meet me there in an hour."

"Okay."

*********

She sat at the café for fifteen minutes, looking out the large window for Officer Duggan. Cars, motorcycles, minivans with kids busying themselves playing video games in the back seat, trucks and a few RVs drove by the window, pulling into the large café parking lot, but Petula didn't see Officer Duggan. She stood to leave just as he walked through the door wearing a pair of faded jeans and a T-shirt.

"Thanks for coming," he told her, bumping her elbow as if steering her back inside the cafe. "And again, thanks for all your help."

Returning to the booth she'd previously sat at, she slid across the seat and asked, "Did you know what was going on when you showed up at Chris' after Paul rammed my RV at the Whooten State Forest?"

"Paul's been in other trouble, but only on a small scale, generally drinking and driving or drinking and getting into bar fights." He shook his head. "Paul used to be a good guy. Fighting in the military special forces changed him, roughed him up. He drinks a lot now. He's not sharp mentally or physically like he used to be. But nothing messed him up as bad as losing his little girl."

Officer Duggan's gaze landed on the table. Looking up, he continued, "His wife passed due to cancer three years into their marriage. Paul raised their daughter on his own after his wife passed. While in the Army, Paul worked his way up to First Sergeant. He did good, was on a good track. Paul's parents kept the little girl while Paul was in the Army. They were an older couple, in their early seventies."

Petula's brow went up. She leaned back into the restaurant booth, pushed her shoulders into the long, cushiony booth chair. "Go on."

"Paul's parents had him late in their lives. They were a nice couple, gave back to the community through charities and other local volunteer work. Paul's their only child. Well," Officer Duggan shrugged. "Paul's little girl was with his parents one weekend. They'd gone camping at the Whooten State Forest." He started shaking his head. "Don't know how it happened, but the little girl – she was six years old – wandered off and her grandparents couldn't find her."

Chewing his bottom lip, Officer Duggan peered at the table. When he looked up again, he twisted his mouth. "We looked all over for that little girl." Lowering his head, he repeated, "She was only six years old."

"So that's why Paul hangs out at the Whooten State Forest," Petula said, her voice drifting off.

"That's likely part of the reason. But," Officer Duggan told her, sitting up. "That's not why he was shadowing you."

Petula frowned. "He did more than shadow me." A second later, she bit back emotion. "Sorry about his daughter. That's sad, so sad. Did the police ever find her?"

Officer Duggan sat across from her in silence for a moment. "Yeah. We found her ten weeks later, reunited her with her grandparents and Paul." He shook his head. "But she was never the same."

"Why? What happened to her?"

"We don't know. Could have been preyed upon by a big cat, a wild dog, who knows? Something spooked her good. Paul paid a lot of money to get her help over the years. Two months ago, his daughter overdosed on opioids." Hanging his head, he added, "Like you said it was sad, really sad."

"That must be why Ashleigh, the woman I met at the state forest when I first arrived, said she'd seen Paul walking into an area labeled "prohibited." Looking at Officer Duggan, she added, "That must be where Paul's daughter was found."

Officer Duggan looked at Petula for a long time, his brow open, his stare blank, before he started shaking his head, one up-down motion after another. "Yeah," he murmured. "It was a hard time for Paul and his parents." He looked across the café, his gaze landing on a spot on the wall. Then, he shifted back to the investigation. "Anyhow, the Service Leaders Retirement Fund you were auditing and asked regulators to do an independent audit on was a resource that Paul tapped into to pay his daughter's mental health, housing and rehab bills. You were the only one pushing for the audits." He signed into, "Based on the investigation, it doesn't look like Paul got any money from the other accounts he was listed on that were involved in the shell scheme." Shaking his head, he added, "Don't even think Paul knew he was listed on those other accounts."

Biting back tears, she said, "I was just doing my job."

"That's true," he nodded. "You did the right thing. No matter what happened, don't ever question that."

"Paul must hate me."

"He doesn't know you, not personally, anyway. Don't even think he knew Dale. Besides, like I just told you, I don't think he had anything to do with the actual shell scheme operations. At the most, he was a benefactor on the Service Leaders Retirement Fund." He shook his head. "He got arrested again, cops stuck a speeding charge on him and took his license after he got picked up in Cranberry, New Jersey a few days ago." Shaking his head, he continued, "I don't think Paul even knew what was going on. Somebody probably just told him that you were destroying the fund, the very resource he used to cover his daughter's rehab, psychotherapy and housing bills. He wanted to stop you, and maybe later, as he watched his daughter suffer then OD, he wanted to get rid of you, make you hurt like he was hurting." He shrugged. "Who knows? Under other circumstances, Paul and you might have become friends."

"Did you know I was coming up North for vacation?"

"We had to have someone on the inside we could trust."

Leaning across the table, she shortened the distance between them and lowered her voice to a whisper. "Did you know I was coming up North for vacation?"

"I can't tell you a lot. There will be a trial."

"At least tell me if you knew about Gloria and James and if you knew that I knew them."

"It was a good connection we decided to work."

She looked at him in disbelief, her brow raised, wide. "You'd studied me. You were just waiting for me to show up."

"We'd studied a lot of people. If it brings you any peace, I only got involved because of the connection to the Custom Accounting Designs Bensalem office."

She massaged her chin. "But you're in Doylestown."

"We have partnerships across police departments. When needed," he nodded. "And this was one of those times when we needed to have a partnership, so to speak."

"So, you were working with the FBI?"

"Only on the Doylestown, Bensalem Custom Accounting Designs office situation."

"But I work in Atlanta."

"But that's not where you started working with the firm."

She turned away from him. "True."

"And I couldn't work on the case with the FBI, not much. I could tell them what I knew for the jurisdiction I worked in. That's all."

She looked at him with her piercing brown eyes, not shifting her gaze, as if she was trying to look through him. "Something tells me you did work that extended outside Doylestown and Bensalem, even if you only did that work online."

He pursed his lips, as if biting back conversation.

She balled her hands into fists and squeezed her eyes closed. When she opened her eyes, she said, "I hope nothing like this ever happens to me or anyone else again."

"I do too. But I discovered one good thing."

"What's that?"

"You're one heck of an investigator."

"I had no choice. I had to do what I needed to do to get peace of mind." She glanced out the window. "Veronica and Arthur must have thought I knew more than I did." Facing him again, she added, "If they hadn't sent Paul and Dale after me, I wouldn't have dug as deep as I did into the client files." Shaking her head, she continued, "They put a tracker on my RV and on my cellphone."

A vehicle backfired outside the café, and she diverted her attention to the window, eyeballing a dirty black and white bread truck, dark fumes puffing out of its exhaust pipe. "It all makes sense now. In some nonsensical way it does," she said after she turned away from the window and faced Officer Duggan.

"You could be right. Maybe Veronica and Arthur thought you were trying to stop the shell scheme. Maybe they feared you would report them to regulators, but you didn't."

Petula twisted her mouth, deep in thought. "What's going to happen to Gloria and James?"

"They're being arrested in Bensalem even as we speak. Imagine that they'll lawyer up."

Petula frowned at the thought of her friends being handcuffed. "Then, what?"

Officer Duggan shrugged. "Hard to say." He pursed his lips and sighed. "Depends on how good their attorney is, but even with a good attorney, they won't just walk," he told her. "Gloria and James hid illegal transactions within work they did with their employers. The case is very layered which is why we needed so much evidence to move forward, and we needed somebody on the inside to get that evidence." He sat back and looked at her. "Your name came up when investigators discovered that you'd asked for an independent audit of questionable records at Custom Accounting Designs." Shaking his head, he said, "I know that Gloria and James are your friends, but I want to see them, every single person involved in the shell game, go down."

"I agree that they must face the consequences of their choices." She sighed. "I'm glad that they have been stopped, even if it wasn't under their own volition. But I can't sit here and tell you that I'm comfortable with my friends going to prison." She glanced out the window. "They should never be allowed to work around money again — ever," she said, her voice raised. "How many people lost money in the scam?"

"As far as we know, two hundred."

Petula bit her bottom lip, fighting back anger. "Just how much money did those people lose?"

"At the bottom end, a couple of thousand dollars. At the top end," he told her, "In the six-figures."

"That's some people's entire life savings."

Officer Duggan raised then lowered his eyebrows. "It is."

"Can't believe Gloria and James could be so selfish, so greedy. How many years do you think they'll serve for their part in this?"

"Judge may give them the minimum sentence, maybe two to three years which they could serve on probation and then order them to repay money they took from others due to the scam."

"Talk about a hard way to ruin what used to be a good life," Petula frowned. "Gloria used to be so smart." She lowered then shook her head. Looking up, her face long, her eyes dim and somber, she said, "I hadn't thought about it before, but now I can't ignore it." She shook her head. "It hurts to think that Gloria and James might have encouraged me to transfer to the Atlanta office so if things went bad, as they have, I'd take the fall or feed them enough information to let them know when to pull out of the shell so they wouldn't get caught." She fought back tears. "It hurts to think they might have been willing to use me, flat out use me." A tear went slowly down her face, which she quickly wiped away.

"Was Chris, the tow truck driver, involved?" she asked, wiping away another tear.

Officer Duggan shook his head. "No. He was just a guy helping you out after your rig broke down."

They sat across from each other for fifteen minutes, discussing the details of the investigation. Then Petula stood to leave.

Officer Duggan walked her to her car. "If it's okay, I'd like to keep in touch with you."

She paused in thought, then told him, "I don't know."

"Promise I won't bother you with anymore legal or criminal cases."

She sighed, turning partly away from him.

"It's a rare day when I meet someone as honest as you."

Although she tried not to, she smiled. "Okay."

Quick and easy, and as if it had always been part of a plan, they exchanged email addresses, and he gave her his personal cellphone number.

He folded the slip of paper she'd written her email address on. Without thought, he flipped the folded paper in his hand, then approached her and wrapped his arms around her. "Thank you so much. I never told you this, but I had a personal reason for bringing them down." He glanced toward the sky, then looked at her. "My parents lost their entire life savings in a shell scheme. I couldn't let that happen to one other person if I could help it, and I could help it."

"Good for you." She smiled. "Do you plan to keep working on the police force?"

"Two more years and I can retire."

"Then, you're going to work two more years," she laughed.

"You bet I am. Are you going to stay in Atlanta?"

She shrugged. "Who knows."

"Well, if you ever want to come back to Bensalem, give me a holler."

"I will."

He hugged her. Just before he released her, he kissed her on the side of the face. Then, he hugged her again.

She held onto him, savoring the strength in his body and the scent of his cologne.

## Read More Books by Denise Turney

Love Pour Over Me

Portia (Denise's 1st book)

Long Walk Up

Pathways To Tremendous Success

Rosetta The Talent Show Queen

Rosetta's New Action Adventure

Design A Marvelous, Blessed Life

Spiral

Love Has Many Faces

Your Amazing Life

Awaken Blessings of Inner Love

Book Marketing That Drives Up Book Sales

Love As a Way of Life

Escaping Toward Freedom

**Visit Denise Turney online** – www.chistell.com

www.ingramcontent.com/pod-product-compliance
Lightning Source LLC
Chambersburg PA
CBHW070925180626
46817CB00003B/1193